Praise for Terence M. Green
and *Shadow of Ashland*

"In Terence Green's haunting novel you'll want to travel every step of the way with the men and women who slip in and out of time's folded shadows."
—Phyllis Gotlieb

"*Shadow of Ashland* succeeds mainly because of Mr. Green's dedication to exploring its underlying themes of redemption, resolution, and homecoming."
—*New York Times Book Review*

"*Shadow of Ashland* is part romance, part mystery, and part 'remembrance of things past.'…The result is a warm, engaging novel."
—*St. Louis Post-Dispatch*

"In *Shadow of Ashland*, Terence M. Green spelunks the Great American Depression and the mystery of a Toronto family's past to emerge renewed into an equally mysterious present. This slender novel transports, clarifies, and touches. You will come away from it moved and subtly, beneficially changed."
—Michael Bishop

"Wonderfully imagined and poetically told.…With Leo's narration as evocative as the pages of a newly discovered family album, this proves a remarkably affecting literary work that the publisher rightly compares to Jack Finney's *Time and Again*."
—*Publishers Weekly*

"The publishers are within their rights comparing this haunting story to Jack Finney's classic *Time and Again*....This is a compelling book one wants to finish at one sitting."

—*Library Journal*

"For a relatively slender book, this novel packs in quite a lot....Most important, it has the ring of truth....A novel that should produce goosebumps and an occasional lump in the throat."

—*The Louisville Courier-Journal*

"Enough quiet wonder and innocence to come pleasantly to life."

—*Kirkus Reviews*

"This is Green's masterpiece....Both thrilling and profound...a voyage back in time and into the human heart."

—Andrew Weiner

"This is a jewel of a novel, sensitively told and filled with fascinating characters."

—*Booklist*

"*Shadow of Ashland* is a magnificent novel, full of characters as real and vivid as the members of your own family, and truths as timeless as the heart. The most important quests are those of the heart. *Shadow of Ashland* is just such a quest—for family, for peace, for closure, for love. It will move you."

—Robert J. Sawyer

*S*hadow
of
*A*shland

Terence M. Green

TOR®

A TOM DOHERTY ASSOCIATES BOOK
NEW YORK

SHADOW OF ASHLAND

Additional copyright information will be found on page 223.

Edited by David G. Hartwell

Cover photo by Don Banks

A Tor Book
Published by Tom Doherty Associates, Inc.
175 Fifth Avenue
New York, NY 10010

Tor® is a registered trademark of Tom Doherty Associates, Inc.

ISBN: 0-812-55526-0
Library of Congress Card Catalog Number: 95-45455

Printed in the United States of America

0 9 8 7 6 5 4 3 2 1

For my brother
Ron
Whom we all miss
Now and Always
1932–1993

Acknowledgments

ACKNOWLEDGING DEBTS AND GRATITUDE UPON PUBLICATION OF A book is something I do with immense fondness. It is a way of saying to the people who have supported, abetted, encouraged, that all our faith has been rewarded.

I would like to thank the Canada Council and the Ontario Arts Council; Doug Gibson, Linda Williams, Paul Stuewe; Rob Sawyer, Andrew Weiner, Lou Fisher, Ken and Judy Luginbuhl, Bill, Judy, and Brigid Kaschuk, Joe and Pam Zarantonello; George Wolfford, Rick Conley, Harold Freedman, Bert Cowan, Bruce Gillespie, Carol Bonnett, Phyllis Gotlieb, Douglas Barbour, and Don Hutchison.

Special thanks to my agent, Shawna McCarthy, and my editor, David Hartwell, both of whom believed in this story enough to get it into your hands.

As always, with love, I thank my family: Merle, for everything, and Conor and Owen for everything else. (Conor deserves special mention this time around for helping me with the ending; he's a better writer than he knows.)

But without Jack, there would be no story.

And without my mother, I would never have known the story.

1

Illusion, Temperament, Succession, Surface, Surprise, Reality, Subjectiveness—these are threads on the loom of time, these are the lords of life. I dare not assume to give their order, but I name them as I find them in my way.

—RALPH WALDO EMERSON
Experience

1

MY MOTHER DIED ON MARCH 14, 1984. IT HAD BEEN INEVITABLE, as all such things are inevitable, and although it had not been unexpected, it nevertheless left me in shock. A large chunk of the past was gone. A large chunk of *my* past.

Gone.

She had been hospitalized just before Christmas. Accelerating arteriosclerosis, recurring strokes, and crippling arthritis had rendered her virtually immobile. She was seventy-four.

I am forty. Soon I will be forty-one.

But these are mere numbers. And what numbers measure, especially those linked to Time, I have never understood. And now I understand them less.

She died, they say, of heart failure.

When I visited her in January, she was rambling. She upset me so much that I cried. There were three other beds in the hospital room, and now I realize that I can't recall anything about their occupants. I only recall how, that day, I got up and pulled the sliding curtains around the bed so that we could be alone, so that I could hold her hand.

Her fingers were welded into the timeless claw of the aged, the skin of her hand stretched thinly across bony knuckles. Lesions and brittle remnants of skin cancers dotted her forearm.

But her eyes . . . It was her eyes—glazed, darting, frightened, the blue diluted as with a watery thinner . . .

"Jack was here," she told me.

I frowned. "Jack?"

"And my father." She nodded. The eyes darted.

I stared at her. Jack was her brother. She hadn't seen him for about fifty years. Her father had died thirty years ago.

"Jack was here," I repeated, finally.

She nodded emphatically. The eyes never ceased their wild circumspection. Her hand gripped mine.

"I told him not to go."

I nodded, understanding.

"But he went anyway." Another nod; a pause. "He was always a good boy. We were good children. Never got into any trouble. Always did what we were told."

I felt the frail bones of her hand, watched the frantic eyes jump about, saw my mother as I had never seen her.

"He gave me this." The hand that I was not holding fell open, and a fresh red rose fell out. It was part of the delirium, I realized. She could have gotten it anywhere.

"He's coming back tomorrow."

I nodded.

Her eyes darted.

I returned the next day. The wildness had passed. In its stead, tubes, suspended from a bottle by her bedside, snaked into her arm.

"How are you today?" I sat down, took her hand in mine.

"Okay." The word was soft and dry. Her eyes, I noted, were steadier.

I tried a smile. "What do you think about all this?" I indicated, with an open hand and a postured inspection, our surroundings: the beds with hand cranks, the crisp white sheets, the gray tile floors, the plastic wrist bracelets.

My mother smiled. She was back from wherever she had been yesterday. "I don't want to die," she said. "Nobody wants to die. But," she added, "I don't want to live like this either."

I nodded, comforted by the clarity of her answer. She understood what was happening, saw no solution, expressed it simply.

How much more time?

"Who would you like to see? Is there anybody you'd like to see?"

Her eyes focused on me calmly. "Oh, yes."

"Who?"

"Jack," she said.

2

MY PARENTS HAD MOVED TO THEIR HOME IN NORTH TORONTO IN 1929. At the time, so I have been told, there were fields all about and a creek within half a block.

The fields are gone; no one is sure today where exactly the creek was. The most general consensus is that it's under the city-run parking lot that serves the subway—which is now the proposed site of the new police station. My father still lives there. Alone.

That afternoon, on my way home from the hospital, I drove to the house where I had grown up—the house I had left twenty years ago. It *looked* like a house that an old man lived in, alone: peeling paint on the eaves, a pitted and corroded aluminum screen door, snow unshoveled in the driveway.

I knew he was in there. He is always in there.

"Tell me about Jack."

My father lit a cigarette, holding it in his right hand. He jammed his left hand in his belt, as was his habit. He is eighty years old now. I am astonished at his white hair, his groping movements, the thickness of his glasses.

"We don't know what happened to Jack," he said.

"I know."

"He left in the nineteen thirties."

I nodded. We sat opposite one another at the green arborite kitchen table. "Why did he leave? What happened?"

He inhaled on the cigarette deeply, then let it expel slowly. "What did your mother say?"

"Nothing much. I asked her who she'd like to see. She said 'Jack.' That's all."

He nodded. "Things were never settled. That's why. Things have to be settled, or they never go away."

I waited. "What happened?" I asked. "Nobody ever told me."

He paused. "I'm not sure," he said.

He lit another cigarette. It was time, he knew, for confidences. "There were only the two of them, you know. Just Margaret and Jack. Jack was two years younger—born in nineteen eleven. We all lived on Berkeley Street together. That's how I got to know your mother. We were neighbors." He smiled, remembering something. "We've been married fifty-four years now."

I smiled. "I know."

"Their mother died when your mother was just a kid. As a result, your mother ended up playing mother to Jack. Margaret adored her father, but the old man, as I understand it, wasn't much help. He always had a big cigar, always boasted. He didn't like me much either," he added. "I remember him saying once, to me—'You don't like me, do you?' I told him that I didn't." He paused. "It's all too bad now. Doesn't seem to matter much either." He lifted the cigarette to his lips and gazed off to the wall behind me.

I waited for him to continue. The smoke spiraled patiently toward the ceiling of the kitchen.

"The old man left Jack and Margaret with his various sisters. He was incapable of raising two kids on his own. He was an only son, in the midst of a flock of sisters, and he was spoiled rotten." My father looked at me. "Always had a big cigar," he said, "but always lived in rented rooms. Those were different times, the nineteen twenties." He sighed. "You want a cup of coffee?"

"No, thanks."

"Me neither. Bad for your heart."

I smiled, looking at the cigarette.

"The two kids lived with the old man off and on from that point. But half the time he was never home. They raised themselves. And Margaret played mother to Jack. They were very close." He switched topic suddenly. "Do you remember the old man? Your mother's father?"

"No. Nothing."

"He died when you were three. Died of a heart attack on the streetcar, on Christmas Day, coming up here to see us. And that was it."

"That was what?"

"The end of the line for your mother. There was no one else. Her mother and father were dead. Her brother had left and hadn't been heard of for years."

"There was you. There was me."

"Yes. But it wasn't the same. The past was gone for her. Do you understand? The past was gone. No one wants to give up the past. At least, no one I know."

The smoke hung in tendrils between us.

His eyes were watery behind the thick lenses. The skin of his forehead was discolored and flaking. He hadn't been eating properly. "Jack was jealous of me," he said.

I listened, without changing expression. I wanted to hear it all. It was time to hear it all. And it was time for him to tell it.

"Your mother married me when she was twenty—when Jack was eighteen. They'd been living alone for a while at that point. The old man had remarried—a girl half his age. The stepmother didn't want his kids. In fact, I was never sure why she wanted him. So he abandoned them for her. This was the 1920s. Family life was strong then. Nobody did those kind of things. At least," he amended, "nobody I knew. So they lived down the street—Berkeley Street—together."

"Where did my"—I paused over the word—"grandfather, live?"

"Out in the west end. Nobody had cars. It was a long way." He inhaled the smoke. It drifted out as he talked. "I guess she chased him because he talked big and smoked a big cigar."

"Who?" I wasn't sure I was following him.

"The girl he married."

"Oh."

"She died three years later, giving birth to their second child."

I was silent.

"It was the nineteen twenties."

I turned my head to look out the kitchen window—to the parking lot that would become the police station. It was beginning to snow.

"So then he had two more kids, and no mother to look after them, and it was all starting again." Then he stared at me, hard. "And he was still living in rented rooms."

"She wants to see him."

"Who?" The thin white eyebrows wrinkled.

16

"Jack."

He had caught the thread again. "He left in nineteen thirty-two, I think. We never saw him again."

"Where did he go? Why did he leave?"

"He left because there was nothing here for him. He was a young man, about twenty-one. He had no use for the old man; he could see through him. When Margaret married me he was alone. I think he felt she had abandoned him. It wasn't fair." He shrugged. "But then, nothing is fair." The cigarette was placed between the thin dry lips once more. "Your mother felt bad. Felt guilty, I think." He looked at me. "Try to see it from Jack's point of view. His mother dies; his father's run off and married this young thing; his big sister marries the guy down the street. It's the Dirty Thirties. Nothing for him here."

I shifted in my chair, crossed my legs.

"He left the country. Left Canada. Went down into the States. Last we heard of him he was in Detroit."

"Why Detroit?"

"Detroit was turning out cars. There were jobs."

"Did he write?"

"Once, that I remember."

"Did anyone try to find him?"

"The Mounties tried to find him."

I raised my eyebrows.

"RCMP came to the door here in nineteen thirty-nine looking for him. Wanted to know where Jack Radey was. He hadn't answered his draft notice."

I waited.

"They never found him either." He drew deeply on the cigarette. "You sure you don't want a coffee?"

I got up and put on the kettle.

"Good. I've changed my mind, too. The hell with my heart."

I stood, looking out the window at the parking lot. The sky was gray and the snow was still falling. A creek, I thought.

Under there. And soon, a police station. Layer upon layer. Impossible to find it.

"When the old man died, they found some correspondence between him and a private investigator he'd hired to find Jack. It was one of the few bright spots your mother could find at the time. The fact that the old man had made some kind of effort to find his own son—that it might have even bothered him—was something he never let any of us know."

"What did it say?"

"The trail had run dry. That's what it said. He was gone."

The kettle began to whistle softly.

3

WHEN THE PHONE RANG THAT EVENING, IT WAS MY FATHER. "I FOUND something you might be interested in."

"What is it?"

"The letter from Jack that I remembered. And a card from your mother to him that was returned unclaimed."

"How old are they?"

"Just a minute." There was a pause. I could picture him pushing his glasses up onto his forehead and squinting at the paper in his hand. "Nineteen thirty-four," he said. "You want 'em?"

The excitement I felt was all out of proportion to the news. There was no reason for it. "Yes," I whispered.

"I'll keep 'em for you."

"I'll be right over." I couldn't wait.

The envelopes were yellowed. The one from Jack was postmarked Feb. 22, 1934, Detroit, Michigan. In the upper right-hand corner, it sported a purple three-cent Washington stamp, and the ironic cancellation imprint: "Notify Your Correspondents of Change of Address." It was hotel stationery. The upper left read: "Return in Five Days to VERMONT HOTEL, 138 W. Columbia, Detroit, Michigan." It had been torn open at the end. It was addressed to my mother, here, at the only address she had ever known after she had married my father.

The other envelope was postmarked Toronto, Ontario, 8:30 P.M., April 29, 1934. It was addressed to Mr. Jack F. Radey, c/o Vermont Hotel, etc., and across the bottom there was a Detroit postmark dated May 3, and a stamped imprint that read: "Return to Writer UNCLAIMED." Somebody else had scrawled in pen: "Try Washington Hotel."

"What's the F. stand for?"

"Francis. Your brother Ron had the same middle name. Your mother's choice."

I pulled the letter from Jack to my mother from the torn end of the envelope. It consisted of four faded sheets of Vermont Hotel stationery, complete with stylized letterhead. In the upper left corner it read: "Phone Cherry 4421"; the upper right bore the announcement: "Rates $1.00 and up." The handwriting was quite legible, and in pencil. It was dated February 22/34.

Dear Margaret:

Received your letter okay, and sure was tickled pink to hear from you. I'm sorry to hear Ronnie has been sick and I hope he is real well and yelling his head off when you receive this.

I must be going "Goof" or something. I was starting to think you had deserted me, and here I had sent you the wrong address. It's funny we didn't get your other letters or the Valentines. They must have been lost in the mail.

Gee—Margaret, I like it real well here. If anything ever happened now that I had to go back I think it would break my heart—no foolin'. I am working in the picture business for the largest and best-paying outfit in town, and I like it.

Do you know that coming here has given me an entirely new slant on life? I seem more anxious to be somebody than I ever have in my whole existence. Things seem to be pretty fair here, and you can live cheaper, and make more money than you can in Toronto.

I received a letter from a friend in Toronto today. The one that phoned you. She said you wished I hadn't come over here with Carmen as he may prove a bit of a bad influence. Well, forget it—he won't; and besides I've met, and mingled with so many fellows who are that way that one more couldn't make any difference. So stop worrying about me being led astray. So far as drinking is concerned, I haven't been doing any. I am too busy making money, and trying to get somewhere. The only thing I'm sore about is that I didn't come here about four years ago. I'd have had a lot more now to be thankful for.

I bought myself a nice new pair of shoes last Saturday and a couple of shirts, etc., and I hope to have a new suit in a week or so. I need one badly.

You know, Marg, the secret of the whole thing is I came over here on my uppers. By the time I had paid Mrs. MacDonald in Toronto, and a few other little items, I was broke. I was determined to come over here, though. The boys I worked with there gave me a rotten deal, and that's no fairy tale. I borrowed a little money from Carmen (that's where he got the idea to come along) and I've paid him back every bit of that right now. That isn't all either—cause I really am going to make something out of myself. I mean it, Marg.

This all may seem strange to you—me talking this way, but I have to tell someone how I feel and you are the only person I feel I can tell without being laughed at for dreaming. This is all just between you and me, Marg. I wouldn't want anyone else to know how I was fixed or what a tough time I had for the first week in Detroit. Everything is going to be okay now, though, and pretty soon I will be able to send you and the children and Tommy something from the U.S.A.

I've been working around Royal Oak—gee, the "Shrine" is beautiful, Marg. I also make it a point to get to Mass on Sunday. Write me real soon.

> Lots of Love,
> Jack

I put the letter down and looked across at my father, who had been quietly watching me. "Have you read this?"

"Yes."

"Where did you find them?"

"In the trunk, at the foot of the bed. At the bottom."

"What did you make of it?"

He shrugged. "Not much."

"He said he worked in the picture business. What did he mean?"

"Margaret told me that he was working as a sidewalk photographer down there. She'd heard this from a friend of his here."

"Sidewalk photographer?" I blinked.

"You know—one of them guys who used to snap your picture, then come up to you and offer to sell you prints when they were developed."

I continued to look uninformed.

"No," he sighed. "I guess you don't know. Polaroids, Instamatics, video replays . . . Of course you don't know."

"I think I've seen them in the movies. Old movies." I smiled. He smiled back. "Yeah. Old ones."

"Doesn't sound like much of a job."

"It wasn't."

"I thought he went to Detroit to work in the car industry."

He shrugged. "I don't know what happened. Sometimes," he said, "things don't happen the way you plan."

I opened the envelope that had been returned unclaimed. Because I had never seen birthday cards from the 1930s, what I found intrigued me. The stationery and greeting card industries, I reflected, had shifted gears significantly over the past fifty years. There were two birthday cards inside—not birthday cards as we know them—but birthday cards of the era: two flat, unfolded cards about ten centimeters square, with elaborate, embossed colored drawings of a bird in a garden and a galleon on the high seas respectively. The former read: "Birthday Greetings Dearest Brother," the other, "To the Nicest Uncle on His Birthday." Each sported a genial epigraph and was signed by my mother, for herself and for the children. On the back of hers was a P.S.—*Why Don't You Write?*

Accidentally, I tore the envelope putting them back. It tore easily.

"And this was it?" I asked.

My father nodded.

"You never heard from him again?"

He shook his head.

"She's going to die, you know."

The eyes behind the thick lenses weakened. "I know."

"She wants to see him."

He shrugged, looked away. "He's gone. He never came back." Then he looked at me. "What can we do?"

I stood up, walked to the kitchen window, stared out at the snow-covered parking lot. Beyond it, the traffic inched along Eglinton Avenue.

2

. . . our faces marked by toil, by deceptions, by success, by love; our weary eyes looking still, looking always, looking anxiously for something out of life, that while it is expected is already gone . . .

—JOSEPH CONRAD
Youth

1

I SPENT EVERY EVENING FOR THE NEXT FEW WEEKS IN TWO PLACES.
First, I would visit my mother; then I would drive to the main
branch of the Toronto Public Library at Bloor and Yonge. There
I would pore over an atlas, copying down names of cities,
towns, communities in and around the Detroit area, and as far
south as Toledo. The litany had become familiar: Windsor,
Pontiac, Wyandotte, Ypsilanti, Ann Arbor, Flint, Lansing, Grand
Rapids—even Saginaw and Bay City—plus numerous others.
Having made my daily list, I would then ask the librarian for
the white pages of the communities' phone books, which were
all filed on microfiche, and seat myself in front of one of the
viewers, scanning them for any mention of the surname Radey.
It was likely, I realized, that he was dead. But it didn't seem
too unlikely that he may have married, may even have had children. The name—"Radey"—proved remarkably uncommon,
which was to my advantage.

My list of names and addresses grew, slowly but steadily.

Eventually, I progressed from the Detroit area to major
cities in general, including New York, Chicago, Cleveland,

Philadelphia, Pittsburgh, Kansas City, Houston, New Orleans, San Francisco, L.A., San Diego . . . I had also begun to realize the impossibility of my self-appointed task. How, I wondered, could I hope to succeed where the RCMP and private investigators had failed? The answer, I knew, was that I probably would not. What I would need was a lightning bolt of luck, pure and simple. There were too many places I could never cover, too many years that had passed.

Yet, I persisted. I wanted to give this to my mother. It was what she wanted. The attempt needed to be made.

My final list consisted of some fifty or so names. A couple were even J. Radeys. One in Kansas City was a John F. Radey.

I wrote my letter.

Dear Sir or Madam:

I am trying to trace a relative—for strictly family reasons—with the surname Radey. I am trying to find Jack (John Francis) Radey, born in Toronto in 1911. His father was Martin Radey (deceased), born 1882 circa Toronto, and his mother was Margaret Anne Curtis (deceased), born Toronto, 1878. He had one sibling—a sister, Margaret, born Toronto, 1909.

Margaret, Jack's sister (now Mrs. Thomas Nolan), is my mother.

If Jack is still alive, perhaps this letter can reach him. Perhaps he married and had children, some of whom might read this. Xeroxing and networking of this letter is encouraged. If this letter should reach anyone with helpful information, please feel free to call me collect, as soon as possible. Any information would be appreciated.

Many thanks.
Sincerely,

I made a hundred copies, mailing as many as I could out into the void.

* * * *

It's not that there were no replies. On the contrary, I received about a dozen cards and letters, most merely assuring me that they could be of no help. A card came from Boston from a family that informed me that their name had been legally changed in 1955 from a long Polish name; the closest I seemed to come was a letter from a lady in Illinois:

My father, Donald, to whom your letter was addressed, died last March, a couple weeks short of his eighty-second birthday. I have two brothers—Todd, in Atlanta, and Paul Michael, of New York.

My father was raised in the Colorado area. We know very little about his family. We never knew any of them. As far as I know, there were no brothers or sisters. As far as I can determine, he had an unhappy childhood and never seemed to want to talk about it—so, I respected that.

I'm sorry that I can't be of some help to you. Good luck in your search.

I wrote to the two brothers.
No answer.

Another brief note arrived as the weeks passed, from Haddonfield, New Jersey.

Dear Sir:
Your letter about Jack Radey was brought to my attention.
A friend of mine who is interested in genealogy suggested that you advertise in the magazine GENEALOGY HELPER, *which is published by the Genealogical Publishing Company, Inc., at 1001 N. Calvert Street, Baltimore, MD.*
You may wish to forward a copy of your letter. They might be willing to publish it.

I sent them the letter. They published it.
Nothing happened.

2

MY MOTHER DIED. I WAS UNABLE TO BRING JACK BACK FOR HER. I
had failed.

Time. It was devouring us all, burying us in stratified layers, impervious to archaeological probes.

The snow melted, leaving puddles of slush that glinted in the
sunshine. Then the puddles dried up and blew away with the
April breezes.

I stood at my father's kitchen window gazing out at the
bulldozers and cranes that were excavating the parking lot—
transforming it into an enormous maw that would serve to support the new police station. In my hand, a mug of instant coffee steamed casually, emitting small rays of warmth.

Behind me, saying nothing, my father smoked a cigarette
with his right hand. His left hand was jammed in his belt.

It was the eighth of May when my father phoned. "I'd like you
to come over."

"Anything wrong?"

"No, nothing wrong." There was a pause. "At least, I don't
think so."

"What is it?"

"A letter came today. For Margaret."

"Who's it from?"

"I opened it." He seemed to be apologizing.

I waited.

"It's from Jack."

I couldn't speak.

"I said, it's from Jack."

"Jack?" My mind was numbed. "He's alive?"

"I don't know."

"You don't know? What do you mean, you don't know?" The words were tumbling out before I could sift them. "You're holding his letter, aren't you?" My voice had become a whisper. It was incredible. Everything seemed incredible.

"Yes, but—"

"But what?"

"Leo . . . Listen to me for a minute." I could hear his breathing as he waited. A second tripped by. Two. Three. "Will you listen?" He was breathing heavily.

I calmed myself. "Yes."

"It came in the mail today. Along with all the usual stuff."

"Where is he?" The question blurted out before I could stifle it.

"It's postmarked Toledo, Ohio."

"He's in Toledo?" It was both exclamation and question.

"I don't know if he's there . . . "

"What is it? What *is* it?"

"The letter's fifty years old, Leo. It's postmarked April thirtieth, nineteen thirty-four. It's written in pencil, just like the other one. The date on the letter is April twenty-ninth, nineteen thirty-four. It was written and mailed fifty years ago, but it came in the mail today. Today!"

I closed my eyes and waited for the explanation to present itself to me. Instead, I saw two birthday cards, one with a bird in a garden, the other with a galleon on the high seas.

My father was strangely composed when he handed me the letter. I wondered whether it was because he had had time to calm himself, or if it was part of the realm of old age to bear surprises with greater dispassion.

In the upper right-hand corner was the same purple

three-cent Washington stamp. The postmark was as he had said.

The letter was two standard 8½-by-11 sheets; atop the date on the letter was the address 117–17th Street, Toledo.

Dear Margaret:

I certainly owe you an apology, and I suppose I owe all the rest of the family one, too. It just seems as though the things I should do, I never get around to, and the ones I shouldn't are always being done.

I got your letter a couple of weeks ago, and I've started to write to you several times. I get about halfway thru and then something happens. How are you all doing, and how is Father?

I didn't have such a good winter, but things are starting to look up now. I lost my car, and just about everything else I had just before Christmas. I had a wreck and was laid up for a while, but I'm okay now, and thinking about another car. I guess I'll be smart to stay away from them for a while, though.

I was sure glad to hear from you. Don't think I'm an awful heel for not writing sooner, but just try and realize what a careless brother you have. I would have dropped you a line at Xmas, but I was in pretty bad shape—physically and financially, so I just lay low and hoped everything would be all right.

I've been in Toledo now for two weeks. How are the children—boy, I'll bet they are getting big. I'd love to see them. If you get a chance to come to Detroit some weekend why not bring them along, and let me know beforehand so I'll meet you there.

I haven't seen anyone you know for so long that I feel like an orphan. I'm still with Hartican. I was away from him for a while during the winter, but started back again. His picture business is still the biggest. I'm working with a chap named McMaster, a real nice fellow. He's been married about a year and a half, and they were blessed with a bouncing baby boy about three weeks ago. He (Mac, I mean) is just ga-ga about the baby. He has me talking like one.

Say—that was a dirty dig about those cards you have for me.

*You'd think you hadn't heard from me in over a year. Send me some
snapshots of yourself and the kiddies. I'm still carrying the one of you
and Loretta in your bathing suits and Ronnie and Anne on the bikes.*

*Say hello to Father and all the gang for me, and write me sooner
than I did you. Try and forgive me for not writing sooner—cause you
know how a fellow slips once in a while. I'm glad to hear Tommy is
doing well and has a new car, and tell Mrs. Nolan I hope she feels
like herself soon.*

I'm "gonna" close now and get some sleep. So long and
Lots of Love,
Jack

I left the letter on the kitchen table in front of my father and
went to the window. In the excavation pit, the foundations had
been poured.

3

THE NEXT LETTER ARRIVED ON JUNE 23. I HUNG UP THE PHONE AFTER
receiving my father's call and drove over to his house in a
daze.

This one was postmarked June 18, 1934, from Bucyrus,
Ohio. The envelope bore the imprint of some roadside inn—
or hotel—or possibly even a motel. I wasn't even certain if such
things existed in the 1930s. Perhaps, I thought, it's merely a
rooming house: "THE HIGHWAY," it read, "on the Nation's Main
Thoroughfare. The Lincoln Highway, Bucyrus, Ohio."

The letter consisted of three sheets of yellowed stationery,
with the same letterhead as adorned the envelope. The upper
left-hand corner boasted: "Modern," the upper right, "Fire-
proof." I glanced once more at the envelope. A red two-cent
Washington was aligned with a green one-cent counterpart. I
read the letter. It was dated, in pencil, June 18/34.

Dear Margaret:

The first thing I want to do is apologize for not writing sooner. You know how I am about letters, though.

I'm still with Hartican of Detroit, but it's been so long since I've seen the office that I almost forget what he looks like.

How are all the folks in Toronto? Say "Hello" to all the gang around the house for me.

Have you been bathing this summer? I suppose Ronnie and Anne are both expert swim champs by now.

There isn't very much to tell, as I've been hitting small towns all along the line. If the next one is as dead as this I'll go crazy.

I don't know where I'm going from here, but we will be leaving in a few days. I'll let you know my next address in time for you to drop a line. Let me know how Father is getting along. I've lost his address.

Things are just about the same with me, I'm not making a fortune but I will one of these days.

I'm "gonna" beat it now and get something to eat.

> *Lots of Love*
> *Your Brother,*
> *Jack*

We were quiet for a long time in the kitchen. Finally, I looked at my father. "Why is this happening?" I asked. I waited for paternal wisdom, for a flippant retort, for exposure of some implausible and outrageous scheme. I watched him frown. and waited.

His eyes were focused on the wall behind me. I glanced sidewise to see what might be there. There was nothing. "Things have to be settled," he said. "Or they never go away."

At home, I dug my road atlas out of a pile of litter in the corner of the basement, and sat down to peruse it.

I found Bucyrus. It was north of Columbus, north of Marion, a tiny speck on Route 4.

Bucyrus. I let the name roll softly in my brain.

He was headed south. Detroit. Toledo. Bucyrus.

On the Nation's Main Thoroughfare. The Lincoln Highway.

Was it happening fifty years ago? Or was it happening now?
I knew the answer. It was both.

He was moving, had moved, is moving, deep into the heart
of America. It was clear. America: the Melting Pot. Canada: the
Event Horizon.

Down the Lincoln Highway. Assimilated. Ingurgitated.

Then and now.

And tomorrow.

The letter that arrived July 5 was the briefest—written on a torn
piece of stationery. It was from Ashland, Kentucky. The hotel
this time was called the Scott Hotel, and the letterhead under-
lined its features: "Fire Proof—Moderate Price—Tub and
Shower Baths." It had been postmarked July 1, 1934.

Dear Margaret:

*Just a line to ask how you are, and how things are going in Toronto.
I am doing pretty well down here. I have my own car now, have had
it for a week, a Dodge Roadster. How are Tommy and the kiddies?
Say Hello to Father for me.*

I'll be in touch.

> *Love,*
> *Jack*

4

I USUALLY TAKE MY HOLIDAYS IN AUGUST. I LIKE THE WEATHER, THE
heat, the end of summer. I usually head north, rent a cottage,
do some fishing. The splash of a smallmouth bass taking a sur-

face lure on an August evening can make the hairs on my neck stand up straight.

This year, I headed south.

Detroit, Toledo, Bucyrus, Ashland.

I had to see for myself.

I told my father. He nodded, sitting in the kitchen.

Outside, the girders rose up out of the pit, giving shape to the police station. The parking lot was gone.

There was no Vermont Hotel in Detroit. There were Holiday Inns, Hyatts, Hiltons. An office building stood on the site where 138 West Columbia would have been.

I drove on.

There was no 117–17th Street in Toledo. At least not any longer.

I took Route 20 east from Toledo to Bellevue, veered south on 269 to 4, then south the last twenty-five miles or so to Bucyrus.

Just south of Bellevue, I passed a billboard advertising the Seneca Caverns, "Popularly known as The Earth Crack." The last thing my eye caught as I drove by was the blurb for the Caverns' "Old Mist'ry River," which "has defied all attempts to measure its depth or locate its source."

Crevices in the earth, I thought. Running in all directions.

Route 4. *The Lincoln Highway*. Bucyrus.

I tried to imagine it as Jack had seen it, leading into the splendor of America, offering him his fortune. A pleasant little burg. Sherwood Anderson country.

I drove back and forth along the main route twice, tasting, searching, looking for more than just the Highway Inn. In some way, I was looking for Jack.

He was not here, though. J.C. Penney was here. So was First

Federal Savings, Rexall Drugs, Halliwell Hardware, Kork 'N' Cap Drive Thru, Radio Shack, H&R Block, and Holiday Inn. Gray-and-white Kiwanis garbage bins were strategically located to polish the exterior.

The Highway was gone. Amish Cheese was still here.

I had no idea where Jack was.

That night I stayed at the Holiday Inn.

The next day, I got back onto 23, and took it all the way to Ashland, Kentucky. At Portsmouth, I crossed the Ohio River.

It was hot and humid, as only August can be.

I stopped at a Burger King for lunch, scanning the local phone books for a Scott Hotel. There was no listing. Instead of "Fire Proof—Moderate Price—Tub and Shower Baths," I was regaled with modern attractions: color TV (twenty-four-hour movies); sauna baths; free in-room coffee; kingsize waterbeds; luxury rooms . . . People stayed at the Ramada Inn in 1984— not the Scott.

I finished my lunch. I had come all this way to see, to try to understand.

Getting into my car, I began to drive, touring the streets casually, my arm resting on the open window ledge.

J.C. Penney was here, too. So was Wendy's, McDonald's, and Arby's. Chevron Gas, McCreary Tires, Midas Mufflers. Dairy Cheer—Home of the Smashburger, ABC Drive Thru Liquors. Sears. The Ashland Oil Company.

I made a haphazard left onto 14th Street from Winchester, and I saw it. *The Scott Hotel.* A creaking rooming house, whose very foundation had shifted, giving it a perceptible list, out of plumb with its surroundings.

The sweat ran into my eyes. At least, I think it was the sweat. I may have been crying. I don't know.

3

So we beat on, boats against the current, borne back ceaselessly into the past.

—F. SCOTT FITZGERALD
The Great Gatsby

1

Opening my eyes, I blinked several times. It was still there, avatar of a bygone era, unassuming and pale.

The Scott Hotel.

I glanced at my watch. It was 3:00 P.M. Easing the car to the curb, I parked.

It was an accident that I had found it. At least, I thought it was an accident.

I got out, walked up to the dilapidated front porch, noted the motionless swing seat tucked in its corner, studied the moon-shaped wells in the three steps before me, and took them smoothly, arriving at the front door. A giant oval of beveled glass, frosted at the edges, was implanted in a heavy wooden frame, laden with innumerable coats of paint, the latest of which was a drab olive green. A cast-iron knocker hung to the right of the glass, chest high. I used it. Then I took a step back, waiting.

When the door was pulled open from within, a small wiry woman in her late forties or early fifties stood in the hallway.

Her eyes were shadowed and squinting. I was unable to see the end of the hall behind her.

For a moment, we merely confronted one another. Then she spoke. "Yes? Can I help you?"

"I'm—" I was at a temporary loss. She smiled, tilting her head to one side. I didn't know what I wanted. I didn't know what to ask. My journey—everything—seemed impossibly foolish.

Yet there were the letters. I had them in the car—in the glove compartment. They were real. They existed.

I tried again. "I'm looking for—Jack Radey."

The smile disappeared slowly, a receding ripple from a stone cast far out into a still pond.

She stood there.

I waited.

"Come in," she said, stepping aside.

I crossed the threshold, entering the past.

We were in a parlor, furnished in leftovers from the thirties and forties. The afternoon sun streamed through partly open venetian blinds into the dim interior, dust motes floating idly in the slanted bars of light.

"Sit down." She indicated the worn, wine-colored sofa, a needlepoint pillow at each end.

I sat, watching how my presence stirred the weightless specks.

She seated herself in a threadbare easy chair, letting seconds elapse as she appeared to gather her thoughts. "Who are you?" she asked, finally.

"My name is Leo Nolan. I'm from Toronto, Canada."

She folded her hands.

"I have an uncle named Jack Radey. My family hasn't heard from him for quite a long time. This was one of his last known addresses."

She listened, without responding.

"I'm on vacation. I'm a circulation manager for the *Toronto Star* newspaper. I'm doing some touring down here in the States. Thought I'd stop by Ashland and see what I could find out—if anything—about Jack."

Her dark eyes clouded. "When did you last hear from Jack Radey?"

"It was a long time ago."

The woman waited.

"Fifty years ago."

Her eyes closed. The dust motes drifted downward, a slow-motion waterfall.

"I'm Emma Matusik," she said. "I know the name. Jack Radey."

I shifted to the edge of the sofa, intent on her words.

"It's from before my time. My parents own the hotel. It isn't much now. But it had its day. There are people who have lived here for years. Mr. Bannerman, for example. Been with us for twenty-three years, last February. Jack Radey did live here, off and on, for quite a while from what I understand."

"When did he leave? Where did he go?"

"You'd have to ask my parents that."

"Was it recently?" I leaned forward.

"Oh, no. Like you said—it was a long time ago. I don't remember any of it. It's all just stories I've heard."

"Stories?"

She hesitated, thinking. "Would you like to speak with my parents, Mr. Nolan?"

"Yes," I said. The calmness of my voice masked the excitement I felt. "Very much."

Her parents, I realized when I saw them, must have been eighty years old. Emma Matusik led them into the parlor, seating them on the upholstered settee at the end of the room nearest to me.

I rose and went over to them, offering my hand. "I'm Leo Nolan."

The old man accepted the gesture, shaking my hand. Then, peering at me, he said, "I know you."

I held his hand, taken aback. "I don't think so."

He squinted, confusion entering his eyes.

His wife had been staring, too, struggling with some memory.

The old man shook his head. "You look like someone I used to know. Name Leo rings a bell, too." He shook his head again. "Was a long time ago."

The old woman spoke. "Maybe your father?"

I shrugged. "Don't think so," I said. "Don't see how." Their reaction to me only left me more curious than ever. Maybe, I thought, I look like Jack Radey. Maybe it's a family resemblance.

Then I looked at them again, at their fragility, their age. Maybe it's nothing, I realized.

The old man let my hand drop. "I'm Stanley Matusik," he said. "This is my wife, Teresa."

"Pleased to meet you." I sat back down.

"What is it we can do for you, Mr. Nolan?"

I glanced at the daughter, wondering what she had told them. She remained silent.

The old man's face had a lined toughness to it, his sparse white hair sprouting in tufts on the sides of his head. The woman did not meet my eyes; although the years had grayed her, she had clearly once been quite striking.

The air in the room was Kentucky still and warm.

"I don't know if your daughter told you. I'm from Toronto, Canada. I have an uncle named Jack Radey. I understand he used to live here."

The room awakened slowly. From an August slumber on the Ohio River, it rolled over, sat up, and crackled like an Ontario fall, the dust falling between us now like autumn leaves.

For a frozen moment, no one spoke. The old woman finally looked up, staring directly at and through me. Emma, the daughter, said nothing, waiting. It was left for Stanley Matusik to break the silence. "Is this a joke? Is that it?" His eyes narrowed as he set his mouth.

"A joke? Good Lord, no." I was taken by surprise. "I don't know what you mean." I looked from one to the other of them, trying to interpret.

The old man put his hand to his chin, spreading his thumb along his jawline. He dropped his eyes, then stared back at me. His wife placed her hand on his free arm, gently.

"Like I know you. Like I seen you somewhere before." He mulled it over. "Who'd you say you were?" he asked.

"I'm his nephew—Jack Radey's," I said, conscious of trying to clear the air of any possible misunderstanding. "He was my mother's brother. My mother died recently, and one of the things she really wanted was to see Jack. Or at the very least, to know what happened to him. She hadn't heard from him in years." The letters, I thought. No. Not yet. "One of the last addresses she had for him was here, at the Scott Hotel. So I thought I'd drop by and see what I could find out—since I was down this way." I added the last part in order to try to restore a casual atmosphere to my inquiries. There were things hovering unsaid on all our parts—ghosts that none of us was dealing with particularly well.

The past.

"Yes," the old man said finally. "Jack lived here." He nodded. "He did indeed."

He placed his own hand atop his wife's, on his arm.

"He left a long time ago."

"When?"

"Nineteen thirty-five."

"Where did he go?"

A shrug. "Not sure." A flicker in his eyes, a candle stirred by a door opening.

I tried another tack. "What did he do while he was here?"

"Took pictures, for a while. Then he worked at the King's Daughters Hospital."

Something new. Something I didn't know. A small wedge, perhaps. "This is in Ashland?"

He seemed to relax, on familiar terrain. "You betcha. Opened during the First World War, as a three-room emergency hospital. The state's just poured eighteen million into it. Gonna be a hundred new jobs at least, they say." He paused. "This old city can sure use them," he added.

"What did he do at the hospital?"

"Worked as a night janitor. Can't remember how long. Six months. A year. Something like that."

"And then?"

"Then he left. He was gone. Like that." He spread his callused hands and stared at me, the candle in his eyes burning cleanly. "You're young. You wouldn't know. It was the thirties, you know. Things like that happened."

I nodded.

We sat in silence.

"I'd like to stay for a while," I said.

They seemed surprised. "How long?" the old man asked.

"A week. Two. Then I'll have to go back."

"Hardly anybody stays here anymore, Mr. Nolan." It was the second time that I had heard Teresa Matusik's voice. There was the trace of an accent, long buried, that lent a richness to the words. "You might be more comfortable at a newer place. More up-to-date."

"Of course we have room," said Emma Matusik, intercepting her mother. "Lots of empty rooms. There's only Mr. Bannerman, Mrs. Kristensen, and Miss Maurice here now—besides us. We'd be honored."

I smiled. "Thank you. I appreciate it." Then I turned to the senior couple and asked it. "If you can remember what room Jack stayed in, I'd like the same one. Is that possible?"

Mrs. Matusik's lips parted as if to say something, but nothing came out. The candle continued to flicker in Stanley Matusik's eyes.

I wanted to go into the past. I couldn't help myself.

2

THE SCOTT HOTEL WAS A RAMBLING OLD THREE-STORY HOUSE. As I was led through it and up to the third floor, I glanced at dark turns in hallways and closed doors with tarnished brass numbers on them, aware of secrets they would not yield. Stanley Matusik plodded ahead steadily, with remarkable stamina for a man his age. When we reached the third floor, he stopped between two doors, numbered 8 and 9.

"Nobody comes up here much anymore," he said. "Too much trouble. Too many stairs." He turned the doorknob of number 8. "Jack stayed in here."

The door swung inward and open.

"Did you ever hear of the 'Battle of Toledo?' " Stanley Matusik stepped aside and let me precede him into the room.

A white-painted iron bedstead. A wooden-veneer chest of drawers. Venetian blinds. A blue upholstered easy chair, facing an RCA black-and-white TV. An oak wardrobe with a mirror inset in the door.

"No," I replied. "I haven't."

The door to a small bathroom was ajar. I could see the wall sink and a towel bar.

"It happened fifty years ago."

I turned to look at him.

"Was one of the reasons Jack left Toledo, came to Ashland."

"I don't know what you mean."

"This room's got its own bathroom. There's a few that do. Was one of the reasons Jack took it, way up here on the third."

"Toledo. Jack," I interjected. "What happened?"

He looked at me. "It was the Depression. In nineteen thirty-four, everybody seemed to be on strike. Must've happened even up there in Canada." He waited.

"It did."

He went over to the chest of drawers, leaned on it. "Toledo was a little Detroit. Automobile parts," he said. "Depression ruined Toledo—especially in thirty-four. It was big news even down here. Willys-Overland—made that jeep—employed thirty thousand people. Went bankrupt. Ohio Bond and Security Bank closed its doors. City couldn't make payrolls." He shook his head. "It was bad." He stared off into space. "Electric Auto-Lite, though. That was the one."

"Why don't you sit down, Mr. Matusik?"

He glanced at me, then at the easy chair. "Might be a good idea." He sat down.

I faced him, sitting on the side of the bed.

"You never heard about it?" he asked again.

"No."

"Was in all the newspapers." He thought about this, then shrugged. "Auto-Lite made lighting, starting, ignition systems. Had contracts with Packard, Nash, Studebaker, Hudson, Willys." He looked at me. "All of them gone now. Strange, isn't it?"

I nodded, as kindly as I could.

"In thirty-four, they got the Chrysler account. A whopper. You could see it coming: lots of product, low wages. Same old story." His eyes focused far away. "They went on strike." He frowned. "Company brought in strikebreakers, special deputies, armed its company guards and stored munitions in the plant."

"Where was Jack in all this?"

"I'm gettin' to that." He continued, lost in his own memories. "There was mass picketing—thousands. City police couldn't handle it all, so the sheriff deputized special police, paid by Auto-Lite. After a few days, the crowd, they say, had reached ten thousand. One of the hothead deputies grabbed an old man and beat him, in front of everybody, and that was it."

I waited.

"The Battle of Toledo. May nineteen thirty-four. It had started. The picketers cordoned off the fifteen hundred strike-breakers inside the factory—kept them there from noon till midnight that day. Deputies in the plant and on the roof fired tear gas, covered an area four blocks around in the stuff. They hurled bolts and iron bars, used water hoses—even some gun-fire. Crowd fought back with bricks and stones. Some fires were set." He shook his head again. "Ugly stuff. Ugly."

I listened, his story coming alive for me.

"Dawn, the next day, the Ohio National Guard was ordered in. Nine hundred men. Eight rifle companies, three machine companies, and a medical unit. Was rainin'. They managed to lift the siege, got the fifteen hundred strikebreakers out. But things were still boilin'. Picketers grabbed a strikebreaker, beat him, stripped him naked. More tear gas. There was actually a bayonet charge. Then, they started shootin'." He became silent and grim for a moment. "Two were killed. Fifteen wounded. Four more companies were ordered in. Largest peacetime display of military power in the state's history. The plant shut down for two weeks. When it opened again, the union had won. They got a five-cent increase. Thirty-five cents an hour."

We were both quiet.

"I know all this because Jack told me. Many times. He was there. Inside." A pause. "He was one of the strikebreakers."

I was speechless when he had finished. To have stumbled about blindly for as long as I had, and now this: a sudden flood of information. Jack's life suddenly taking shape—a shape I could never have guessed.

A strikebreaker.

I must have looked dazed, for the old man broke the silence. "I know what you might be thinkin'." He scratched his head. "Don't be too hard on him."

I still hadn't spoken.

"He was a kid. Hell, we were all just kids. Hadn't thought things through. But we all needed money. Needed it in a way you can't even imagine."

"He never mentioned any of this in his letters to my mother."

"Course he didn't. He was ashamed. He saw what takin' a man's job could lead to, saw what he'd done. He'd ended up pitted against other fellows just like himself—guys tryin' to get by, feed themselves and families. But he was just like them— needed the money. That picture-takin' stuff—didn't lead to nothin'. Who could afford to get their picture took?"

I sat in Jack Radey's room, listening to Stanley Matusik expand and recast this bubble from the past, increasingly awed at his perceptions. His face grew more animated.

"You can't judge. Any of us might of done the same thing."

It was true.

"Fat cat named Miniger owned Auto-Lite. Drug huckster. Coal operator. Used to sail around Lake Erie on a yacht. They said he was worth ninety million dollars." He shook his head in disgust. "And the union thought they'd won when they got thirty-five cents an hour."

I crossed my legs, leaned back on the bed, thinking.

"And two men died."

Like separate drumbeats, his last words echoed from the past.

"His job as night janitor at the hospital."

"Good, honest work," said the old man. "Stupid, dull, boring work. But honest. Jack didn't have many illusions left." He paused. "None of us did."

"Tell me about it?"

"What's to tell?"

I wasn't sure. "How long did he do it?"

"Don't know. I'd have to think about it."

"Weeks? Months?"

"Months. I already told you."

I waited for more.

"They paid him for eight solid hours of work, but Jack said he could get all his chores done in two or three hours. Lots of times he came home and slept. Others, he'd just wander around."

"Wander where?"

"Around. Go for walks."

"In the middle of the night?"

"Sure. What else was he gonna do?"

I didn't know. I had no idea.

"Nineteen thirty-three," he said. "Roosevelt became president. Inherited Hoover's mess. There were twenty million unemployed." He considered me anew. "You were born in the forties, right?"

"Yes."

He shook his head. "Still look awful familiar to me." He frowned. "Must be the likeness to Jack." He shook his head again, continuing. "Anyway, born in the forties, you've never seen anything like it."

He was right.

"Ever hear of Barbara Hutton?"

The name rang some sort of bell. Unable to place it, though, I shook my head.

"Woolworth heiress. Got forty-five million dollars for reaching the tender age of twenty-one. Newspapers were full of it. Five-and-dime business was booming. Profits were twenty percent, net." He fell silent, retracting a memory more finely. "Teresa worked as a salesgirl at Woolworth's." His eyes hardened as the detail he had been seeking crystallized: "She made eleven dollars a week.

"The thirties." He touched his forehead. "Christ. What a mess." He looked at me. "You better let me quit this ramblin'. Get my blood pressure up." He began to rise.

"Don't let me stop you, Mr. Matusik. This is exactly why I'm here."

He assessed me quietly. I realized that what I had just said belied my earlier contention that my visit was some sort of casual afterthought—a sidebar to a haphazard vacation.

He was standing now, silent.

I stood, too.

"Maybe," he said, "we can talk some more after dinner."

The door closed behind him.

Until I slowly exhaled, I hadn't realized that I had been holding my breath.

I was alone in Jack's room.

I had traveled the Lincoln Highway, had come to Ashland.

On a small table at the side of the bed was a silent, round alarm clock, both hands frozen at twelve. I picked it up, turned it over, cranked the winding mechanism, and listened as it began to tick.

Exhausted, I lay back on the bed and closed my eyes. I drifted briefly into the warm cavern of sleep, dreamless.

4

And because they were lonely and perplexed, because they had all come from a place of sadness and worry and defeat, and because they were all going to a new mysterious place, they huddled together; they talked together; they shared their lives, their food, and the things they hoped for in the new country.

—JOHN STEINBECK
The Grapes of Wrath

1

WHEN I WOKE, I WAS SWEATING. I'D FALLEN ASLEEP ON A HOT AUgust afternoon, in a room with air as still as its furnishings.

I checked my watch. 4:40 P.M.

I pushed myself to a sitting position, groggy and with a slight headache, and stared at the closed window. I got up and opened it. The warmth that greeted me was as stifling as that within, but differed in that it was alive, smelling like a city: fragments of oil, pavement, and steel.

I leaned forward on the ledge and looked out at Jack's world.

At an angle across the street was a church turret. To my right, a bit farther away, was what appeared to be a large bank or trust company. When I peered farther left, I could see a theater marquee that read "Paramount." And below, for someone from Toronto, traffic appeared to be nonexistent.

I stood back, assured by the ordinariness of it all.

The only sound in the room was the ticking of the bedside clock that I had wound earlier. It read one o'clock. I had slept for an hour.

Picking it up, I adjusted it to read 4:40, uncomfortable at yet another blatant specter of differing timelines. It was something small. But it was something that I could control. And understand.

Twenty minutes later, I stood on the corner of Winchester and 14th, letting the late afternoon sun beat down on me. The church turret that I had seen from my room belonged to the Calvary Episcopal Church, an elegant Gothic structure. The bank farther right was the First Bank and Trust Company: commercial dignity with financial stability. And the Paramount Theater to my left seemed to round off the triad of the spiritual, the realistic, and the imaginative bridge between the two spheres quite nicely.

In no hurry, I began to walk.

F. W. Woolworth Co.

My ambling had brought me to a point across the street from the store, and recalling Stanley Matusik's anecdote, I was curious.

I crossed the street and went inside.

If the store didn't date back to the thirties, then it was in its own time warp. Large fans hung from the high ceiling at intermittent points throughout the store, stirring the heat lethargically. The fluorescent lights in rows about them hummed like insects. And as I strode forward, the long slats of the hardwood floor creaked with age.

Stopping, I pictured Teresa Matusik, young and pretty, toiling behind a counter for $11 a week.

As in most Woolworth stores that I could remember, there was a restaurant area to one side, consisting of a long counter and swiveling red-and-chrome chairs. There were only two customers there; the waitress was sitting on the end seat reading a magazine.

After I sat down, she glanced up at me, then returned to her magazine, giving me time to read the wall signs behind the counter that served as menu.

Liver and Onions
Vegetable & Potato
Coffee or Small Soda   2.99
Grilled Chopped Steak with Fried Onions   3.49
Freshly Grilled Hamburger Platter   2.79
Club House Sandwich with French Fries
Coffee or Small Soda   3.79

It was intriguing. It must have been thirty years since I'd eaten in a Woolworth's, and that had been the one that used to be on the northwest corner of Yonge and Eglinton, before the days of the shopping center.

My mother had taken me there on occasion. French fries and a fountain Coke. Or a chocolate sundae. A treat.

Assorted Pies   .99
Baked Fresh Daily Muffins   .50

And yet another sign read "Muffin of the Month & Coffee," with a movable slot for the variable flavor—this month's was "Cherry"—all for the bargain price of 79¢.

The waitress, thirtyish and pleasant, approached. "Can I help you?" Her pencil hovered over a yellow receipt pad.

I nodded toward the signs. "What do you recommend?"

She smiled. "To eat? For dinner?"

I smiled back.

"Someplace else," she said. A small laugh.

A half laugh of my own. "You could be right."

She was appraising me. "You're not from around here, are you?"

I shook my head. "Just visiting."

"Well." She drew the word out, thinking. "If you like liver and onions, that's what I'd get. Lots of folks don't like them, though."

"I like them."

"That's my recommendation then." She smiled. "First time in six years I've been asked for my opinion. Just goes to show, that if you live long enough—"

"—anything can happen," I finished.

"But seldom does." She grinned and moved down the counter to the stove.

"We close at six," she said, removing my plate, "or I'd recommend, without you even asking, any of our pies."

I glanced at the clock atop the Dinette sign behind her. The hands were perfectly vertical, up and down. Then I took note of her name tag.

"Thanks very much, Jeanne." I drained the coffee and put four one-dollar bills on the counter. "Next time."

"You bet." She smiled.

I felt her eyes on me as I left, friendly, curious.

Just like I was trying to be about Ashland.

Just inside the entrance to the Boyd County Public Library on Central Avenue, I found a pay phone and placed a collect call to Toronto. My father answered and had the good sense not to debate with the operator.

"Dad. It's me, Leo. I'm in Ashland."

"Good for you. How is it?"

"Hot. Interesting. I found the Scott Hotel."

"Jesus." He was quiet.

"Everything okay?"

"We got another one."

"Another what?"

"Letter."

The heat shimmered through the glass doors.

"It's from Jack. From the Scott Hotel."

"I can't believe this." Things had just begun to seem mundane, the way they should be.

"Don't believe it. It's here, though."

I breathed deeply, my heart beginning to speed up. "What's the date on it? When was it mailed?"

"Like the others. Fifty years ago."

Looking at my reflection in the glass, I began to feel dizzy.

"It's dated August third, nineteen thirty-four."

"Read it to me."

"I don't read so good."

"You read fine." I pressed my lips together tightly. The heat was beginning to make me sweat. My mind was buzzing.

He cleared his throat.

I pictured Jack in the room as I listened.

Dear Margaret:

I'm still here in Ashland, and have a nice room with its own bathroom and lots of privacy. I'm still with the picture business and doing real well. This is a good place to live, and I hope I can stay awhile.

Mac has gone back to Detroit. He couldn't stand being away from his family any longer. It was real hard on him, so I don't blame him a bit.

There's a radio downstairs where I'm staying, and in the evening the people here all listen to it for a while. Everybody listens to Amos 'n' Andy, and we heard all about that family up in Ontario, the one that had the quintuplets (I think that's how you spell it). Everybody here figures I must know the family personally cause we all live in Ontario. You know how it is.

The other big news on the radio was the killing of John Dillinger, with the Lady in Red outside the Biograph Theatre, by the G-Men last month. Apparently he was watching "Manhattan Melodrama," a cops and robbers story starring Clark Gable and Myrna Loy. Because it was in Chicago, I thought about you and Tommy. Remember how you told us that when you were in a speakeasy in Chicago, people bragged about how John Dillinger used to come there?

Has Tommy got his vacation yet? Are you going down to Port Dover? I'll bet the kids can hardly wait.

There's a movie house real close, and I even took out a library card. A fellow's got to do something with his spare time.

Gee, Marg—it sure is hot here, but I don't mind. It sure beats the cold.

Say hello to all the gang for me. I'm getting sleepy, so I'm "gonna" go now.

> *Lots of Love*
> *Jack*

Through the receiver, I listened to the crackle of the miles and the years between all of us.

2

I STEPPED THROUGH THE DOORS AND STOOD ON THE HOT PAVEMENT, staring at the public library.

I even took out a library card.

Hands in my pocket, I walked back toward Jack's room.

The parlor was empty when I got back. Before going upstairs, I scanned it with new eyes. It had struck me as justifiably quaint when I had sat here earlier, but it wasn't until now, until after listening to Jack's latest letter, that I noticed the radio.

I crossed the room and knelt down on one knee in front of it. It was a true Depression item: a piece of wooden furniture, about three feet by two feet, with a cloth mesh over the speaker at the bottom, an arrow pointer on a semicircle band that indicated the station, and three round, protruding knobs on its face. The brand name on it was King. There was a brass letter opener and a glass ashtray on top of it.

I ran my fingers along its side.

"Nobody listens to it much anymore."

I turned to see Teresa Matusik standing in the hall entranceway.

"Jack wrote to my mother about how everyone here would gather around and listen to the radio in the evenings."

She looked surprised. "He did?"

"Wrote about listening to 'Amos 'n' Andy.' About the Dionne Quints. About the news of Dillinger being gunned down in Chicago." I paused. "He wrote a good letter."

"I didn't realize." She came in and sat down on the settee. I stood by the radio.

"He liked it here a lot."

Her face clouded with the past. "I liked Jack," she said. "Everybody did."

I sat down.

"Hard to explain it to folks nowadays. Got TV now. But back then, that there radio," she pointed at it, "went on like clockwork every week night at seven. Everyone, including President Roosevelt, listened to 'Amos 'n' Andy,' from seven to seven-fifteen. None of us found out till years later that it was two white fellas doin' black voices. All you could do was hear 'em."

I let her talk, hoping for more pieces to slip together.

"I used to serve tea. We'd have six, eight, ten people down here every evening. Radio was on from seven till nine. Burns and Allen. Al Jolson. Rose Marie. The Green Hornet. Kate Smith. Right up to the war, Mr. Nolan. Most folks who stayed here were folks just working for a few weeks or months here or there in town. This is a steel, oil, and coal town. Dirty work, but it was work. Lot of the men stayin' here were glad to work a hundred hours a week for fifteen dollars. Some of them came from farms where they'd been eatin' wild greens, violet tops, wild onions, forget-me-nots, wild lettuce, and weeds. There were kids to feed. We tried to treat 'em nice here, make their stay pleasant. It's nice to hear, even now, that Jack liked bein' here. After all," she said, "he was just like all the rest of them. Just tryin' to get by."

"What is it you really want, Mr. Nolan?"

"Pardon?"

"Really."

I shrugged, wondering how to explain.

"Jack Radey hasn't been here for fifty years. When he was here, he was just one of dozens passin' through."

"But he stayed awhile here."

"Lots did that."

I didn't know how to tell her about the letters. "This is the last address that I have for him."

"But he's gone. Long ago. It's a big world. He could've gone anywhere. You're wasting your time."

I studied her face, lined with valleys, scoured by drought, healed with soft rains, then watched her fold her hands in her lap as her daughter had done. I glanced at the radio once more. "Does it still work?"

"The radio?"

"Yes."

The wooden shell hid dust-covered tubes that lit and warmed slowly, an ancient carriage of corroded metal cubes and spools and looping wires.

"Good," I said.

"Evenin'."

I turned to see Stanley Matusik standing in the parlor entranceway.

"Evening, Mr. Matusik," I said, standing briefly as I spoke, then sitting back down.

He came in and sat beside his wife. "Been thinkin' about a lot of things since you showed up here, young man."

I smiled at being considered a young man.

"Things I haven't thought of in years and years."

"Not all bad, I hope."

"Bad. Good. Them words don't seem to fit. Just things that happened. The way they happened. Things you can't change. Things you lived through. You know what I mean?"

"I think so."

"Mm." He sighed, put his hands on his knees.

My eyes strayed to the aging, patterned wallpaper, the child's portrait in the elongated oval frame above the two of them. I wondered if it was Emma.

"Some years I can't keep straight in my head. Just a blur. Others, they just seem to stand out clean and polished. You got years like that?"

"Yes, I do." I thought of 1969, the year I got married, and of 1972, the year it ended. I knew '84 was going to be one of those years, too.

"Thirty-four, thirty-five. They're pretty clear to me. We'd just bought this place. A big step."

"I can imagine."

"My father was a coal miner. Died young. Didn't have nothin'. Teresa's folks were more genteel."

She clucked her tongue. He smiled.

"They owned the Blossom Restaurant here in Ashland," he continued. "That's where I met Teresa. Workin' there. Lamb and oxtail stew, with a coffee, fifteen cents. Remember?"

She nodded. "Yes."

"Her parents loaned us the down payment for this place, but shouldn't have, 'cause they had to close their own restaurant down not too much later. Teresa ended up workin' at Woolworth's. I tried a few things myself. We all did." He filtered memories behind his eyes, retrieving them. "Had to." Turning to Teresa, he said, "I told him some about Jack and that business in Toledo, this afternoon. Young people got no idea."

Teresa looked at her husband. "Mr. Nolan and I were talking about folks listening to the radio back then."

He almost smiled. "I remember the first radio I seen. Jimmy Robinson had it. He didn't have any electricity. We hooked up a coupla car batteries. Got 'Mr. Keen, Tracer of Lost Persons.' Was a serial." He nodded. "Remember it well." A pause. "Radio was big. No question. 'Death Valley Days' on Fridays, 'Chase and Sanborn' show on Sundays."

" 'Chase and Sanborn'?" Coffee was all that came to my mind.

"Music. Comedy. Don Ameche, Edgar Bergen, Dorothy Lamour, Armbruster's Orchestra. Like that. Sunday evenings."

"Jack's Sunday was different," said Teresa Matusik. "He went to church most weeks. He was Catholic. Then he'd listen to something else." She slowly separated her own memories.

Stanley looked at her.

"Father Coughlin."

Stanley looked stricken. "I'd forgotten," he said.

"You know who he was?" she asked me.

I shook my head.

"Broadcast every Sunday from the Shrine of the Little Flower at Royal Oak, Michigan. Started the National Union for Social Justice. Five million listeners signed up within two months. Real angry speeches, especially against Roosevelt. People were ready to listen to what he had to say."

"Haven't thought of him in years," said Stanley.

"Would you like a cup of tea, Mr. Nolan?"

A fragment of Jack's letter from Detroit—the one my father had unearthed in the trunk—floated upward in my mind. *I've been working around Royal Oak—Gee, the "Shrine" is beautiful, Marg.*

I smiled. "That'd be nice."

I sipped the tea. It was hot and strong.

"Ever hear of Pearl Bergoff?" asked Stanley.

I set the cup in its saucer with a solid click. "I'm beginning to think I haven't heard of very much, listening to you two."

"He was the king of the strikebreakers. In thirty-four, it wasn't just Toledo. Was truckers in Minneapolis, tire manufacturers in Akron, longshoremen in San Francisco, millhands throughout the South. Auto industry was shakin' in its boots. Was everywhere. Bergoff ran a multimillion-dollar business recruitin' and providin' scabs for businesses. Worked out of New York. Hired guys to scan out-of-town newspapers for signs of strikes brewin', then he'd dispatch one of his sales staff to peddle his services. He'd ship 'em a small army, outfit 'em with machine guns, billy clubs, tear gas, whatever." He paused. "Jack got caught in his web, up there in Toledo."

Another piece slipped into place. "I see."

"Pinkerton Detective Agency was another favorite of the fat cats. Chrysler liked them lots. Places like GM and Chrysler— they paid their top men two hundred thousand dollars each, paid their workers less than a thousand dollars. Would pay millions to Pinkerton and others, though, to keep it that way. Was unbelievable." He looked at me. "You have," he said, his voice tightening, "no idea how desperate we were gettin'."

No, I realized, I didn't. But I was beginning to see. There was a rough outline taking shape, with my uncle dangling down on a long thread into the dark heart of it all.

"This here's poor country, Mr. Nolan," said Stanley Matusik. "Kentucky, Tennessee, West Virginia. Ohio might be a little better'n most—bit more industry. Nobody gives us nothin'. Back then, it was like the song said: the rich got richer and the poor got children. Simple as that. Somethin' had to be done."

I waited.

"Was the Wagner Act. You heard of it?"

"Yes, I have." It was something I had heard of, finally.

"It was because of what happened everywhere in the country in thirty-four that it got hammered out and signed in thirty-five. It was a start. Management finally had to bargain with unions in good faith. Couple of years later, there was a minimum-wage law—after more strikes—like the one Teresa got involved in at Woolworth's." He reached, held her hand, squeezed it. "You a union man, Mr. Nolan?"

I nodded. "Newspaper Guild."

"Then you know."

I thought of my father, who had worked right up into the 1950s with no pension, no benefits, working evenings, Sundays. "I think so," I said.

Another abrasive edge from the past surfaced, scraping soundlessly against what I had been hearing. "Did Jack have a car?" I asked.

"Car? You must be kiddin'. None of us had cars." Stanley took a long sip of his tea. "Chevy half-ton pickup would've cost six hundred fifty dollars. Could've used one, too. A Pontiac coupé would run about six hundred dollars. Packards were over two thousand dollars." He thought back. "Knew a fella bought a used twenty-seven Lincoln in thirty-four. Paid a hundred tweny-five dollars for it. Nah," he said. "Jack didn't have no car."

I rubbed my forehead.

That night, alone in Jack's room, I took the letters from my suitcase and reread the parts I had remembered.

Toledo: *lost my car . . . had a wreck and was laid up for a while . . .*

Ashland: *Have my own car now . . . a Dodge Roadster . . .*

I stared out the window onto the warm streets of Ashland, picturing my uncle, an iron bar gripped tightly in his fist, trying to stand on the right side of the line.

5

*Look ahead into the past, and back into the future, until
the silence.*

—MARGARET LAURENCE
The Diviners

1

WHEN I WOKE THE NEXT MORNING, I LAY IN BED FOR A WHILE STAR-
ing at the ceiling. My gaze tracked the layers of paint above me
to where they met the wall, slid down the vertical surface,
over cracks and filled-in nail holes, then fell sideways to the
bathroom door, across it like a shadow, resting finally on the
window through which I had peered the night before.

I folded my hands behind my head, stretched in the clean
sheets.

The whining drone of a heat bug rose high in the sky, sting-
ing the warm air.

The bathtub was an old four-legged model that had been fitted with a shower attachment in more recent times. Part of it
consisted of a chrome hoop over the tub, suspended from the
wall and ceiling, from which the shower curtain was hung. I
opened the tiny window in the bathroom, started the water,
and stepped inside the plastic wraparound, letting the warm
spray center between my shoulders. The water ran in a stream

from my chin as I looked upward, watching the steam rise and roll toward the window.

A new day, I thought. The old and the new, everywhere about me.

I sat down on the red-and-chrome swivel chair and looked down the counter.

Jeanne glanced up from her magazine and met my eyes. A small half smile was slow in coming. Flipping the magazine over to save her place, she sauntered toward me, pencil poised over her receipt book. "Can't believe you're back."

"Must be a creature of habit."

"Once is a habit?"

"A habit I started when I was a kid. You can blame my mother. People blame them for most things, now that I think of it." I caught myself, as a picture of her came back to me—an image of her about my age, her dark hair braided and wrapped around her head—actually in the Woolworth's at Yonge and Eglinton, with me in tow.

"In the five-and-dime with Mom."

I nodded. The memory could not be shared.

She shrugged. "So what'll it be?"

I'd been studying the signs. "Says you got an all-you-can-eat breakfast for three forty-nine, until one P.M."

She smiled. "Can be quite a bargain, you know how to do it."

"How should I do it?"

"Don't touch the pancakes."

I waited for more.

"Nor the sausages."

"What does that leave?"

"Bacon, eggs, toast, juice, coffee. Nothing much we can do to them. You'd be safe."

"How many do I get?"

"Like it says. How many you want?"

"Why don't you load up a plate for me? You decide."

"You look like you could use some fillin' up." She stood back, appraised me. "I'll go easy on the cholesterol, though."

"You've got a good eye."

"An' I got two of them," she said, watching me with one of them as she scrawled on her receipt pad.

"You ever heard of Barbara Hutton?" I asked.

She refilled my coffee cup.

"Can't say that I have."

I nodded, lifted the cup to my lips.

"Should I have?"

I shook my head, swallowed.

"Sounds like a movie star."

"Does, doesn't it?"

"Well?"

I looked at her.

She waited.

"It's not important."

She rolled her eyes. "What'd you mention it for then?"

"I don't know."

"What is it, a big secret?"

"No. Not at all."

"Well?" She waited.

"She used to own Woolworth's."

She looked surprised. "This one?"

"All of them. In the thirties."

"The thirties," she said, emphasizing the last word.

I smiled. "That was before your time, right?"

She put a hand on her hip. "Just barely." Then, with a bit of coyness: "Was it before yours?"

"It used to be. But," I said, "I'm not so sure anymore."

* * * *

"I'm Leo, by the way."

She cleared away my dishes, leaving the coffee cup. "Where you from, Leo?"

"Toronto. Canada."

"Jeez. So you come all the way from Canada to eat at Woolworth's in Ashland. You escape from a mental institution or something?"

I chuckled. "I'm on vacation."

"So this is the big trip, is it?" A fake whistle. "I don't know about you, Leo. You got your day pass on you?"

She was funny. I checked her finger. No ring. When I looked back at her face, she was smiling at me. Her face had lines, but they were good lines, travel lines to places others hadn't visited.

My own face, I knew, was etched with a singular, preordained route.

"More coffee?" she asked.

I nodded, smiled.

A fellow's got to do something with his spare time.

I walked the streets.

Around noon, my legs told me it was time to stop. I was exploring a sturdy little industrial community, invaded by franchises and brand names.

In a drug store, I bought a paperback novel—the new Robert Daley cop thriller, *The Dangerous Edge.* I'd read *Year of the Dragon* and *Prince of the City.* It was exactly what I wanted. The all-you-can-eat breakfast was still with me, so I contented myself with a can of Coke and found a shaded bench, in the spacious park back of the library, on which to sit and read for a while.

The park was flat and grassy, with the exception of three protruberant mounds, about ten feet in height, a hundred feet or so off to my left. I focused on their geometric incongruity, wondering if they had any meaning, in a world of incongruities.

High up in the elms, the heat bugs whined.

Later that day, just inside the public library, I dialed the phone again.

In Toronto, my father answered.

I waited to hear it.

"Mail brought another one."

I was beyond surprise. I had almost expected it. "Read it to me."

He cleared his throat. "It's dated August twenty-first, nineteen thirty-four."

"Mom's birthday."

"That's right."

Dear Margaret:

This will reach you after your birthday, so I apologize for that. But as you can see, I didn't really forget it, I just didn't get organized. Knowing me, I'm sure you can appreciate that. So Happy 25th! Where does the time go?

Things are going swell for me down here. I'm making pretty good money, and making some good friends, too. Maybe I'll be able to treat everyone back home soon to something nice. I'd like to have enough to send the kids something from the States for Xmas.

I've been to the movies a lot here. The Paramount's almost right beside me. The folks around here tell me it was built in 1930 using a design that Paramount Pictures used for their model theater at the Chicago World's Fair two years ago. Gee, Marg, it's beautiful. You'd love it. Last week I went and saw James Cagney in "Public Enemy," and this week I saw "I Am a Fugitive from a Chain Gang," with Paul Muni. A really funny thing happened at the movies this week. You know how they get someone to come up on stage before the movie starts and draw ticket stubs for prizes? Well, would you believe it—they drew my ticket as one of them, and I won a free hairdo at a local beauty salon. Everybody laughed when I went up to collect the prize. I must admit, it was pretty funny and I laughed, too. I didn't know what to do with the prize, so I gave it to the lady who owns the Scott Hotel.

The Paul Muni film was very moving, Marg. See it up there, if you and Tommy get the chance. I still don't have Father's address. Is he well?

Write me when you get a chance, okay?

"Gotta" go and take some pictures. You know how it is.

Say "hello" to everyone for me.

Love,
Jack

2

MIDAFTERNOON, I STOOD FACING THE CLIFFS ON THE OPPOSITE shore, watching barges filled with iron ore and petroleum wend their way up the Ohio to Cincinnati. I was struck by the width of the river, the distance to the Ohio side. Like everything else, the closer you got to it, the greater it seemed.

About four o'clock, I returned to the hotel and went up to my room. Tired, I lay back on the bed and let events and information sift together in my head, wondering what to do next. I heard the front door open and close as somebody left the building. Going to the window, I looked down and saw Stanley Matusik heading off, slowly, down the street.

Even after he had reached the corner and disappeared from sight, I stayed there, leaning on the ledge.

I knocked gently on the Matusiks' door.

Teresa Matusik opened it. "Mr. Nolan," she said.

"Sorry to bother you, Mrs. Matusik."

"Stanley went out for a walk. Emma's doing some shopping."

"Could I talk to you?"

She looked startled.

"Just for a few minutes," I said.

Some hesitation. Then she shrugged. "I guess so." She considered asking me in, then changed her mind. Shutting the door behind her, she led me into the parlor.

I sat on the wine-colored sofa opposite her.

She waited for me to begin.

I had considered every evasive tactic, every manipulative rhetoric, but had abandoned them all. "Mrs. Matusik, if you'll forgive my directness, I'd like to ask you something."

She folded her hands in her lap.

"It sounds kind of silly."

She listened intently. "Ask away."

"Did Jack Radey ever give you a voucher or a coupon for a free hairdo in a beauty salon? Back in nineteen thirty-four?"

Her dark eyes became watery and her lips parted.

"It would have been August of that year."

The silence filled every crevice of the room. I could hear my heart beating.

"Yes," she said, quietly.

My heart pounded with the rush of blood.

Her face softened, a memory crystallized. "How did you know?"

The letters were real, then. They were true. Teresa Matusik sat across from me, as perplexed as I was. "He wrote a letter to my mother. He told her."

"Your mother. His sister."

"Yes."

"I didn't know he was writing to her." She looked down. "I didn't know enough about him at all." Her hands remained folded.

73

I tilted my head. "I don't understand."

"Stanley doesn't know."

I was quiet.

"He wouldn't have liked it if he'd known I'd accepted such a gift from another man. It would've undermined him. But," she said, "I couldn't resist. I guess I was weak." A fragile smile. "Such vanity. I was just a girl. It'd been years since I'd had my hair done in a beauty shop. Years. So I accepted it. But I kept quiet about it, and made Jack promise not to tell anyone around here. I didn't know he was writing to his sister." She shook her head. "Didn't know at all."

My heart was slowing down. I sat back.

From deep within her aging body, she looked out at me. "I felt real pretty afterwards. First time in quite a while." She nodded, remembering. "Real pretty."

"I won't say anything."

She was grateful. "Thank you." There was more she wanted to say, but it wasn't going to come. Not now. Not yet.

At ten minutes to six, I sat down at the curved counter and stared at Jeanne.

She put her hands on her hips. "You here for the big dinner? We close in ten minutes. Can't be done."

"I know. It's okay."

She looked at me curiously.

"I don't know anything about you, so if I'm out of line, just tell me. I'm a big boy. I can take it." I wasn't much good at this stuff. "But if you're not involved with anyone, and feel so inclined, I was thinking you might join me for dinner. My treat. I'd enjoy the company."

There. I'd done it. I'd learned long ago: expect nothing, and you won't be disappointed. But every now and then, you've got to try.

She was clearly a subscriber to the first part of my theory.

Her slightly openmouthed expression was one of complete bemusement.

She started to speak, then stopped.

I sat there, trying not to feel like a schoolboy.

"You're a real mover, Leo from Canada," she said, finally.
"Been a long time since I've had a dinner date. Especially with
an exotic traveler." She stood back, eying me playfully. "Tell
you what."

"What?" I asked.

She brushed a strand of hair from her face, tucking it behind her ear. "We'll start with a coffee and talk about it. There
are complications."

At least it wasn't "no." I nodded, approving. "One step at a
time," I said.

We went to a diner, half a block away, and sat in a booth.

She stirred some sugar into her coffee. "I don't even know
your last name."

"Nolan. Leo Nolan."

She tapped the spoon on the cup's rim, then placed it in the
saucer. "And you don't care what my name is."

"I care. Very much. I'd love to know your name."

She put her tongue in her cheek and looked at the ceiling.
"Right," she said. "I'm Jeanne Berney."

"I knew I'd like the name."

"Just how lonely are you, Leo Nolan?"

I chuckled, then began tending to my own coffee. The
woman across from me was a veteran of the male-female game,
and like veterans of anything, she survived because of instincts
and some kind of innate sinew. I liked survivors. I wanted to
be one. "Nothing abnormal. Just medium lonely. Stranger in a
strange land."

"You married?"

"No."

"Honest?"

I nodded. "Honest."

She thought about it. "Guys traveling. You never know. Guy your age, isn't married, but likes women. Makes a woman wonder." She sipped her coffee.

"Wonder what?"

"What the story is."

"The story," I said. "The story is that I'm not such a hot item. I was married once. Back in the early seventies. I've been divorced for a long time."

She pressed two fingers against her cheekbone and studied me. "Any children?"

"No."

"Girlfriend back home?"

"Look at me. What's the hot item?"

She smiled.

"See what I mean?"

She conceded it.

"Since we're doing inventory, what about you?"

She let several seconds lapse before finally answering. "I'm not married. But I've got a kid. Little boy. He's ten. You like kids?"

"I think so."

"Good." She formed a ring around her cup with the thumb and index finger of each hand. " 'Cause if you want to eat with me tonight, you got to include him."

I smiled. "It's a good deal," I said.

"And I pick the spot."

I must have looked as bemused as she had, back in Woolworth's.

"Don't worry," she said. "We got simple tastes."

The sun, even after six, was still hot as we walked.

"What's your son's name?"

"His name's Adam."

"What does he do all day in the summer while you're at work?"

"Plays with his friends. I hope," she added. "Lots of baseball."

"Who looks after him?"

"My parents. That's where we're going now."

"Nice of them."

"It's mostly my mother," she said. Then: "Where you staying?"

"The Scott Hotel."

"Don't know that one."

I smiled. "I'm not surprised."

She walked beside me unselfconsciously. I guessed that she had thickened at the waist in the last five years or so, but her figure was still quite feminine, without attracting attention. I considered my own shape now, aware of how my chest had somehow begun to slip toward my beltline of late. I had thinning hair and new creases in my face. We were both, I realized, safely anonymous, and it made me feel comfortable to be with her.

"What do you do in Toronto?"

"I work for the *Toronto Star*. It's a newspaper."

"Doing what?"

"Circulation manager. They divide up the city into districts, and there are a dozen of us. We look after home and newsstand delivery for our district. Handle accounts, routes, like that."

"They need twelve of you?"

"Toronto's a big city. Three million people."

"I didn't realize."

We waited at a traffic light. "How big's Ashland?" I asked.

"About thirty thousand."

I thought about it. "Could a person get lost here, permanently?"

"What do you mean?"

"Could he come here and hide forever?"

"Don't know if you can do that anywhere." She looked at me. "You thinkin' of doin' that?"

I shrugged. "No," I said. I squinted into the sun, shading my eyes to peer across the street. "I was thinking of someone else."

The light changed. We crossed the road.

We went up the steps onto the porch of the modest frame bungalow on Carter, east of 30th, and opened the wooden screen door.

"Mom?"

"In here."

We went inside.

Mrs. Berney was a small, portly woman in a large housedress. She looked at me curiously.

"Mom, this is Leo Nolan."

I held out my hand. "Pleased to meet you."

She accepted the gesture. "Nice to meet you." Her hand was warm.

Jeanne glanced around. "Where's Adam?"

"Down at the lot. Playin' some baseball with Kenny."

"Good. Thanks. See you tomorrow morning." She kissed her mother on the cheek, squeezed her shoulder, and headed back toward the front door.

I followed. "Nice meeting you, Mrs. Berney."

"Pleasure." She placed her hands on her hips and watched us as we went through the screen door. I thought I saw a smile on her face.

The lot turned out to be a vacant, fenced-in parking lot, adjacent to a boarded-up factory. There were two kids in it—one hitting fly balls, the other catching and fielding them. What made it challenging was the weed growth and the intermittent six-inch-high, six-foot-long cement parking dividers still in place.

We watched for a minute. The kids didn't seem to notice either the field's limitations or us.

"Adam!" Jeanne raised her arm.

The kid in the field put his hand over the visor of his cap, shading his eyes more fully, then raised his own arm.

"Who's Kenny?" I asked, indicating the tiny batter.

"Neighbor. They spend a lot of time together."

Adam Berney trotted over, a tiny imitation of every major league fielder headed for the bench that he had ever seen on TV. His mother bent down, gave him a quick kiss on the side of the head. Ignoring her, he waved to his friend, who waved back.

"Adam, this is Mr. Nolan."

"How you doing, Adam?" I held out my hand.

He looked out at me from under his Cincinnati Reds cap, a squint of uninterest, then shook my hand. "Fine," he said.

"We're going to dinner with Mr. Nolan."

He looked from one to the other of us.

"But you get to pick the place." His mother waited.

He brightened. "McDonald's," he announced.

I looked at Jeanne for a signal of some sort. She smiled at him, then turned to me, still smiling.

"McDonald's it is, then," I said.

"All right!" Adam Berney pounded his tiny fist into his baseball glove for emphasis.

3

"WHAT ARE YOU GOING TO GET?" SHE ASKED ME AS WE GOT IN line.

"Not sure." I was reading the menus behind the cashiers.

"I want a Quarter Pounder with cheese, fries, and a Coke,"

announced Adam. "And one of them." He pointed to the plastic Smurf figure that was the 59¢ throw-in.

"You got kids," she said to me, "you got this menu memorized."

We sat down. The eyes from under the baseball cap peered up at me inquisitively.

"Nice glove," I said, trying it on for size. "Got a good pocket."

"Cost me forty-nine dollars. On sale. I just about died," interrupted his mother. "Can you believe it? Forty-nine bucks?"

Adam glanced from one to the other of us, stuffing the french fries into his mouth with his fingers.

I shifted my index finger outside the leather at the back for support, flexing it open and closed. "Good quality," I said. "Good value."

She looked surprised. "Really?"

I nodded. "Will last a lifetime. He can give it to his son someday. It'll still be good. In fact, it'll be better. Worked in."

Adam beamed a sudden smile.

I undid the cord at the end of the baby finger, pulled it tighter, then retied it.

"It's a beauty," I said, handing it back to him.

There was no answer, but he continued to smile.

"Who do you like on the Reds?" I asked.

"Dave Parker," he said. "Mario Soto."

"Great players," I said. Biting into my burger, I confessed, "I've never had a Big Mac."

"You're kidding," said Jeanne.

I shook my head, chewing.

"Don't they have McDonald's in Toronto?"

I nodded. "Yup. But I don't go there much." I had always thought there were usually too many kids there.

"You from Toronto?" It was Adam's first real attempt to communicate with me.

I stopped chewing, pleased. "Yup."

"You watch the Blue Jays?"

"Sometimes. Who do you know on the Jays?"

"Dave Stieb. Lloyd Moseby."

"Good men," I said.

"Jays are pretty good this year," he said. "For a change."

"And the Reds are kind of disappointing, aren't they?"

"They got Pete Rose back, though." His face was hopeful.

"It's a good move. He'll help. Bring some zip to the club. They can use it."

Adam hollowed his cheeks, sipping his Coke through the straw, not taking his eyes from me.

Jeanne sat back, watched the byplay, smiled.

"So this is a Big Mac," I said, taking another bite, chewing, considering.

We stopped outside a two-story frame house, painted pale blue. It still wasn't dark.

"This is it," she said. "We rent the upstairs."

The three of us formed a comfortable triangle on the sidewalk. Jeanne placed her hand on her son's shoulder.

I sighed, looked around, put my hands in my pockets. Forty years old, I thought. You never quite get the hang of it. "Thanks for the company," I said.

Jeanne smiled. "Thank you," she said. "It was very nice."

"Thanks," said Adam.

I tugged his cap down over his face playfully. He giggled, pushed it back up. "It's Detroit this year, I think. All the way. Morris, Trammell, Gibson, Hernandez. Who's gonna stop them?"

He listened, all ears, the big glove dangling from his small left hand.

I looked at Jeanne. "I'm here for a bit longer. Maybe we can do it again."

"I'd like that."

She glanced at the upstairs window. "I don't think it's a good idea to invite you in this evening. Work tomorrow, and Adam and I still got some things to tend to."

"That's okay. I understand."

I held out my hand. She took it warmly, firmly.

As I returned, hands in pockets, to the Scott Hotel, I squinted into the sun that warmed my face and chest. Behind me was a long shadow with soft edges that stretched out from my feet, moving with me, touching the darkness at my back. I stopped before turning the corner at 14th Street when I noticed the sun high up on the church turret across the street.

Then I turned, saw that the shadow was gone, saw the long street, cracked pavement and cement, dwindling off into the past.

6

A chill night breeze came whispering down from the depths of the valley, and suddenly the place was full of ghosts—shadows of men alive and dead—my own among them.

—CHARLES NORDHOFF AND JAMES NORMAN HALL
Mutiny on the Bounty

1

Sometimes what we become and where we end up is of greater surprise to ourselves than it is to others. Plans get skewered. Logic falters. We become human, terribly so, stumble, try to recover, fail, choose another direction and move onward, shadow and sunshine, the road behind us disappearing, the one ahead unknowable.

It was 1:00 A.M. I could not sleep.

The streets of Ashland led in all directions as I walked in the summer night.

Ashland, like all places, is a very tangible entity. It has a skin that you can feel brushing you as you stand still, fingers that stroke you as you walk, a voice that whispers to you at the edge of hearing. And at night, the entity hums like an electric generator.

"Lots of times he came home and slept. Others, he'd just wander around."

Its dark warmth blossomed in misted, prismatic halos, perfectly still about the streetlamps overhead.

My footsteps were silent.

* * * *

Life, to a great degree, is about loss. Our experience tells us this. We lose our hair, our teeth, our muscle tone, the acuity of our vision, the smoothness of our skin; we lose money, books, pencils, keys, shopping lists, gloves, umbrellas; our cars rust out, neighbors move away, we discard the favorite slippers with the flopping soles.

Our hope is that it can be contained to the externals, that the damage to our internal landscape can be minimized.

When my son was stillborn, I lost a part of myself that was so large and that went so deep that I feel its absence to this day. When the marriage subsequently died, my optimism lapsed.

I lost the house I lived in. Standing in the hallway of the house that I had shared with Fran for three years, staring for the last time at the furniture, the array of photographs on the walls and end tables, the pine baseboard that I had lovingly installed in the living room, the rugs, the drapes: the memory of it flashes like a snapshot in my head. I see myself closing the door, hear it shut with a solid click, feel my chest constrict. Then it is gone.

I lost part of my self-esteem. I lost friends. I lost the illusion that I was somehow immune to the reversals of modern life.

When my mother died, I lost my youth.

There is a sequence that the mind and the soul can accept. It is a form of entropy: the tendency of all things to collapse, given sufficient time. It is when the sequence is disrupted, when that which has not run its normal course and span collapses into disorder, that we feel the steel lance in our hearts, see the vacuum open to swallow us. This happens when youth precedes age into oblivion.

It happened when my son did not live.

It must have happened when my mother's little brother disappeared.

Yet I know that I have not fully matured, even yet, because I know that there will be more.

Am I happy? To have suffered the loss and death of loved ones, one would have to be a bit obtuse to consider himself happy.

I am content. I am wiser.

Life is interesting.

At night, the King's Daughters Hospital on Lexington Avenue is any hospital, in any city.

Beneath a streetlight a cab driver sat, his left arm propped out the window, a newspaper folded against the steering wheel. He eyed me briefly as I stood with my hands in my pockets, looking past him to the building.

A young man came out the front door, stood a moment, oblivious of both of us. At a distance, and in the dark, his features were blurred. Early twenties, I guessed; the short sleeves of his white shirt hung from his elbows as he lifted his hands to run them through black, curly hair. He turned and walked with an unhurried gait up the street.

Watching him, the humidity and stillness seemed to ring in my ears.

I began to follow him. I could offer no reason even to myself for doing so. It just began to happen. Like everything else.

For almost a year following the end of my marriage back in the seventies, I experienced a kind of clinical depression, hovering on the edge of nervous breakdown. I lived in a small studio apartment by myself, went to work daily, read books, watched TV. I went out seldom—had little interest in it. Some friends, who I now realize were the most perceptive and sensitive, sought me out, since I rarely sought them out.

For a while, in the evenings, I took to playing solitaire at the dining table while the television played in the background. The rhythm of the cards was soothing—mindless yet fascinating. It became a Zen-like activity: repetitive, calming. And with the periodic and irregular flow of numbers, colors and suits, with the random serving of patterns, success and failure, came insights that helped me get through it all, helped steer me back into the mainstream of life.

I saw with clarity that there was no reason for many things. There were only permutations, combinations, ebb and flow, flood and drought. The cards sometimes fit together in a sudden burst of accessible harmony, during which all things happened with ease; then just as quickly and randomly, they sealed off further progress. It was something I needed to see at that point in my life, and I learned to accept *satori* where it could be found.

The young man walked on ahead of me through the night. Breathless, almost dazed, I continued to follow.

The blanket that is night can change everything. Vision. Thoughts. Assessments.

With silent footsteps, the air thick, we sauntered through the pools of incandescent haze spilling down from the streetlamps, him leading, me trailing, a hundred or so feet apart.

I dared not develop the thoughts that had begun to stir, like leaves eddying, in my brain. They made no sense.

The young man with the dark curly hair continued onward, oblivious of my presence. When he crossed the deserted street, and headed north on 14th, I stopped momentarily, a rush of adrenaline making me light-headed. Then I, too, crossed in the stillness, and fixed my gaze on him as we headed north, my thoughts swirling.

We were headed in the direction of the Scott Hotel.

*   *   *   *

I thought, for some reason, as I walked, of my father in Toronto, sleeping as ever in the house we had all shared. I remembered the night sounds of my youth: my brother's teeth grinding in the bottom bunk; the moan of a nightmare coming from my grandmother's bedroom—one of many that awakened us with increasing regularity in her final years; the subdued voices, muffled, of a disagreement between my parents, indistinct yet unsettling, from behind their closed bedroom door.

Just as suddenly, I remembered being inside that bedroom with my parents, listening to them laugh as I cut out risqué cartoons from my father's *True* and *Argosy* magazines, absorbing the distinct smell of the hardwood floor on which I lay, as I pasted them into the scrapbook my mother had bought for me to occupy my child's attention span.

Then it was winter, and I was walking along Eglinton Avenue, going home from second grade, my slippers in a plastic bag, my black rubber boots with the tops folded over on my feet, beside an enormous snowpile bulldozed at the edge of where the buses turned into the subway station. I climbed the hill of snow, tumbled, burrowed, felt the cold crystals slide into my boots, then became drawn into my own world of fantasy and experiment. I buried my slippers in a deep hole on the far side of the snowpile, knowing they were wrapped in plastic, certain that I could retrieve them the next morning on my return route.

I dug for days afterward and could not find them. And it remained a mystery that I confronted on a daily basis as I passed the spot, baffled. I did not tell anyone. I got by indoors at school by remaining quiet, in my heavy, extra socks.

And I recalled how in the spring, when the snow melted, the plastic bag lay in the midst of charcoal slush and road salt, intact, materializing as if from another world.

I placed the bag in a garbage can on the way home. I never

told anyone. I had outgrown the slippers and could not grasp their reappearance. They belonged to the past.

He stopped outside the Scott Hotel.

Behind him, I slowed, holding my breath.

He glanced up at it, hands in pockets, then moved on.

I followed.

He turned right and walked along Winchester, stopping again to stare at the monumental First Bank and Trust Company building.

My eyes strayed from him to gaze at the tall first floor of the edifice, to appreciate its decorative windows, its columns set in antis between wide corner piers. Then I tilted my head back, absorbing the upper stories, noting the broadly projecting copper cornice at the top.

When I looked back at where he had stood, he was gone.

The street was empty in both directions.

I stood, stunned, alone, the Ashland night flowing over me, the world silent. A fog entered my head, then lifted, leaving my vision, at that moment, cut with the brilliancy of a diamond.

A magic place sought years later seldom materializes.

When I was a teenager, there was such a place nestled in the rocks on the opposite side of Ashbridge's Bay on Lake Ontario. You could sit there for hours looking across the lake, down to where Woodbine Beach curved out onto the water. The rocks tumbled and fit in just the right shape and position. There was privacy and beauty.

I used to take a girlfriend there and while away the hours. Ducks would swim by. Geese, gulls, terns. They would get the scraps from the picnic lunch.

I can picture it clearly in my mind, even now.

Yet when I tried to find the spot some years later, I could

not. Several places looked similar, but none of them quite right. There were more or fewer rocks. The path was wider, narrower, covered with different growth. Always something.

I found another spot.

I don't know where the other one went.

The next morning, after showering and dressing, I walked back to the spot where I had last seen the young man. In the bright daylight, surrounded by the street sounds of traffic, it seemed quite a different experience. Gone was the intensity of vision, the preternatural sense of awareness; in its place was the ordinary, the expected.

About me, people engaged in the business of the day.

I stood on the sidewalk, at the exact spot where I had last seen the man standing. I looked across at the First Bank and Trust Company building, playing out the moment before he had vanished.

The building told me nothing.

Below me, though, the sidewalk was broken, where it had sunk over the years. The shallow depression and cracks at my feet marked his disappearance.

The earth, I thought, and looked down. It's as though it swallowed him up.

I drank coffee in a diner, staring through its smeared windows out onto the street.

2

EMMA MATUSIK OPENED THE DOOR TO HER FAMILY'S LIVING QUARTERS when she heard me come in the front. "Mr. Nolan?"

I looked up.

"Message for you. Phoned while you were out." She handed me a piece of paper.

I expected it to be from my father.

It was from Jeanne. There were two phone numbers. One said "Work," the other "Home."

I smiled.

Then I saw Emma Matusik eyeing me curiously. There was something else that she wanted to say. "There's some stuff," she began, "in the back here, that you're welcome to. Couple of years ago, we bought some things with the idea of updating some of the rooms, but the plan never got too far." She shrugged. "My father just wanted an excuse to buy some of the modern gizmos, I figure. Nobody's stayed here long enough to make updating the premises much of a priority for quite some time now."

She went back inside her apartment. I followed her through the open door.

It took two trips to carry them to the third floor. I lugged the small bar fridge up to room number 8 first, then returned for the microwave on the second trip. They were both brand-new; the Matusiks hadn't even bothered to remove them from their cardboard boxes.

I set the microwave on top of the chest of drawers and the fridge on the floor beside it, plugged them both in, then sat back in the blue easy chair to enjoy the spectacle of my new domesticity.

A fellow, I thought, could stay here quite a while.

And Emma, for some reason, seemed to want me to.

"This one's dated September thirtieth, nineteen thirty-four." The line carrying my father's voice from Toronto was clean and clear.

I listened to the words, and their echoes.

Dear Margaret:

I've been here for more than three full months now, and it's really beginning to feel like home. Me, a Southerner! Can you believe it?

Still trying to get ahead, Marg. I guess I'll always be trying. In fact, I'm involved in something here that has lots of promise, so just keep your fingers crossed. It's what I've been needing to get started— just that little start-up stake. Some of the fellows here at the Scott have got a project that's very interesting. The man who runs the hotel has agreed that it makes sense, too, and with his help, something is really possible. But enough of this. I'll try to keep you posted, if things work out okay.

Like I told you, Marg, I've met lots of interesting people, and seem to be able to keep busy. But there's still some time to fill, and I've been reading a book called "The Moon and Sixpence," by W. Somerset Maugham, which I got from the library. It's about a fellow named Charles Strickland who abandons his home and family and travels to Tahiti in order to paint. Somebody asks him in the story if he's never bored or lonely, and he replies "It is evident that you do not know what it is to be an artist." Heck, I guess I don't know what it's like either, cause I can't figure why he'd leave his wife and kids behind. But, and I have to admit it, there's a part of me that understands exactly what he's doing and why. The rat race for money and staying one step ahead of the guy behind you is enough to wear anyone down.

But I'm no artist, Marg. Heck, I can't even paint the side of a house.

It's just past dinner time, and I'm going with a friend to the movies tonight. "King Kong" is playing at the Paramount. I hear the ape gets a bad deal. It should be fun, and I can sure use some fun.

Say "hello" to everyone for me, and send me Father's address, okay?

Lots of Love,
Your Brother Jack

There was nothing to say.

Jack, I thought.

Where are you?

At Woolworth's, I bought a microwavable plate, a drinking glass, a mug, and a set of stainless steel cutlery.

Before leaving, I went and sat down at the counter in front of Jeanne. She was serving a customer, but caught my eye and smiled—a genuine, pleased smile.

"How you doin'?" She leaned forward on her hands.

"I got your message."

She shrugged. "Pretty bold of me." Her hair fell out from behind her ear. "But I figured, what the heck, you seemed like a decent guy. And decent guys don't grow on trees. I know."

"I'm glad you called."

She looked relieved. "Listen," she said. "I was wonderin' about tomorrow evening?"

I waited.

She licked her lips, then continued. "Seeing as how you took us to dinner, I was hoping you'd let me take you to dinner. Just the two of us. Show you some Kentucky hospitality. I know a nice place."

I smiled, knowing what it took to make such an overture. I'd made many of them myself. Too many. "My pleasure," I said.

She stood back and straightened, her confidence restored. "Great. My mom offered to keep Adam for the evening." The loose strand of hair got tucked back behind the ear. "You know where I live?"

I nodded once, still smiling.

"Give me time to get home, get changed. Can you come by at seven-thirty?"

"I'll be there."

Now it was her eyes that smiled. "I can't believe I'm doin' this."

"Feels good when it works out, doesn't it?"

"It surely does," she said, nodding. "It surely does."

At a 7-Eleven, I bought a jar of instant coffee, a container of orange juice, six Pepsis, some bananas, milk, cream, sugar, and a box of Cheerios. Then, to diversify my cuisine, I tossed in two frozen dinners and a frozen pizza.

At ABC Drive Thru Liquors, I bought six cans of Miller Lite.

I had my Robert Daley novel, the TV in my room, and I wouldn't be seeing Jeanne until tomorrow night.

Like Jack said, I thought.

A fellow's got to do something with his spare time.

I microwaved the frozen dinner and drank two cans of Miller Lite while I watched a ball game on the TV. Then I fell asleep on the bed during the news, my novel open on my chest. When I woke, Carson was ending, and groggily I rose and switched it off.

Nighttime. At last. I went to the window and drew it in through my pores.

I had been waiting for it.

At 1:00 A.M., I was standing across from the King's Daughters Hospital, the night warm and sultry, the street silent and calm.

He came out the front door, just like last night.

I held my breath.

The only sound was that of his footsteps as he strode down Lexington, Central Park on his right, some of the fairer manors of Ashland on his left.

It was a replay. He turned right, heading north on 14th Street.

I followed.

For the five blocks between Lexington and Winchester it was as though the rest of the world had been sealed off, while we, the two of us alone, moved through a blackness that crackled with possibility.

When he stopped at the Scott, I stopped. And when he turned along Winchester, I turned, too.

Across from the First Bank and Trust Company building, he paused, put his hands in his pockets, and stood in contemplation. Again.

I watched, hypnotized, afraid to lose him a second time.

Then he turned and met my gaze.

We stared at one another, without fear, without suspicion. The air was truly alive now, and I felt my heart beat with a wonder and certainty that it had never known.

Jack Radey stood before me, a young man in his early twenties. I knew it was him. I could tell by the jaw, the cheekbones, the dark, black hair. He was a Radey—my mother's brother.

My uncle.

We stood on Winchester Avenue, in Ashland, Kentucky, that hot night in August, some twenty feet apart.

He smiled. He put his hands in his pockets and smiled, full of wonder and delight. And youth.

It was a perfect moment, one of the few that we are allotted in our lifetimes—a moment when the eons needed to transform coal into diamond contract with the purity of quicksilver.

Nineteen thirty-four or 1984?

They were the same. For that brief instant, then and now were in the palm of my hand.

And when I blinked, he was gone, as I knew he would be, and I was once more alone in the night.

7

*I have an idea that some men are born out of their due
place. Accident has cast them amid certain surroundings,
but they have always a nostalgia for a home they know
not. They are strangers in their birthplace . . .*

—W. SOMERSET MAUGHAM
The Moon and Sixpence

1

THE NEXT MORNING, I SPOONED INSTANT COFFEE AND SUGAR INTO my mug, filled it with water from the bathroom tap, and microwaved it to steaming. I stirred in cream until it brought the temperature down to a drinkable level, poured myself a bowl of Cheerios and some orange juice, and broke a banana off from the bunch.

I pushed the blue upholstered easy chair over to the window, set my breakfast on the ledge there, and sat down to eat, staring out at the sun warming the church turret on Winchester Avenue.

Jack, I thought. Jack Radey.

"Gonna be a hot one."

Pulling the door shut behind me, I turned to the source of the voice. Sitting motionless on the veranda swing, in the morning shade, was Stanley Matusik.

"How are you this morning?"

He nodded. "As ever."

I walked over beside him, then half sat against the railing, facing him. I had the feeling that he had been sitting here, waiting for me.

"So what do you think of Ashland?"

I squinted, looking out across the street, into the glare. "Nice." Then I looked back at him. "Very nice."

The silence that hovered between us for the next half minute was a good one, unhurried, patient.

"Any more on Jack Radey?" he asked, finally.

I squinted once more into the brightness of the morning, away from the veranda. Then I turned back to meet the weathered eyes staring at me. We shared another silence. Then: "He's here, somehow," I said. "It's all here, somehow."

Stanley Matusik continued to stare at me. He dropped his gaze and nodded. "Like everything else," he said. "There's things that're there all the time. All's you've got to do is clear your head to see 'em."

A heat bug whined and the air shimmered off the hot pavement.

"That building there." I pointed along Winchester.

Stanley's gaze followed my finger.

"The big one."

I watched his face, studying its lines.

The wrinkles at the corners of his eyes straightened, a memory floating to the surface behind them.

I waited.

He sat back, quiet, reflective. Then he looked at me. "Bank," he said. "Why?"

I shrugged. "Seems impressive."

We were both silent for a moment.

"Anything special about it?" I asked.

His brow furrowed, and the seconds flowed by like a meandering stream. "Bank's a bank," he said.

Looking at its height, I considered this. "When was it built?"

"Nineteen twenties."

I leaned back against the railing once more, listening.

"Was the Ashland National Bank then. Didn't make it through the Depression, though. Like lots of others. Was taken over by the Second National Bank in thirty-two, I think. Changed again only about four years ago. Now it's the First Bank and Trust Company." He looked at me. "Bobbin' and weavin'. Got more lives than some cats," he said.

I let him continue.

"Not all banks was like that." He was rolling now, and the opening that I had probed grew larger. "By late thirty-two, more'n six thousand banks had locked their doors. That's over one-quarter of the banks in the whole country, Mr. Nolan. Nine million people saw their life savings disappear like smoke in thin air while they slept. Happened lots 'round here. Lots," he said. "Happened to four people who used to live here back in thirty-two. Mrs. Donohue was one of 'em. Widow woman. Had their money in a bank little farther down the street there"—he nodded—"and they put locks on the front doors, closed the place up. Mrs. Donohue had 'bout fifteen hundred dollars in a savings account, which she got from her husband's insurance policy, along with six hundred fifty dollars of her own money, saved over thirty years of dressmakin'. Gone. That was it. She left. Had to go live with relatives. Nothin' left but to accept charity. Same with the others." He shook his head, remembering.

"But that one." He nodded toward the bank that we could see, the one that rose some ten stories above the ground, towering over the downtown core. "That one's still there."

I sat back, wary of the raw, exposed nerve that I had uncovered.

"And Jack?" I asked suddenly.

Stanley seemed to start from the name. Then he firmed. "Jack's gone," he said. And his eyes clouded, angry, frustrated. "We don't know where."

I said nothing. In my head, I saw Jack smiling, alive and young, in the pristine night.

Across from the Scott, beside the Calvary Episcopal Church, was the Ashland News store. I browsed, intending to buy a newspaper, maybe a souvenir. I found postcards celebrating Kentucky in general, some imported from Lexington and Louisville, but nothing with an Ashland logo; the same was true of T-shirts, pens, key chains—you name it. Ashland did not advertise itself.

It had no identity in a larger world.

I bought the *Daily Independent*—the Ashland paper—tucked it under my arm, and went back out into the sunshine.

Between 14th and 15th, on the north side of Winchester, construction was fully under way for the Ashland Plaza Hotel, "luxury accommodations in the heart of the city—opening September, 1985." The architects' drawing stood in stark contrast to the Scott, a stone's throw away.

I looked from one to the other, at odds across the street. The past and the present, momentarily crossing paths, I thought.

Again.

On the northwest corner of Winchester and 17th was what used to be a post office. The cornerstone read 1916. In its windows were For Lease signs.

And in 1934? I wondered.

Is this where you mail them from, Jack? Is this it?

At the Jolly Pirate Donuts on the corner of 20th, I had a coffee and doughnut and read the newspaper. Nothing seemed out of the ordinary, either here or in the world at large.

Behind the library at 17th and Central, I sat once again on the bench in the park. As before, the three large mounds—perhaps ten feet high—in the otherwise level grassland caught my eye; this time, though, I sauntered over to have a closer look.

There was a wooden plaque that had seen better days marking them. Indian mounds, it said, dating from the Adena period (800 B.C.—A.D. 800). Opened in 1870 by a Dr. Montmollen, they were burial sites. Ashland, it appeared, had been the site of an ancient village, and the entire area was speckled with graves. These had been restored.

The underground world, I thought.

Surfacing, receding.

Surfacing.

I ate lunch in McMean's Pharmacy at Winchester and Judd Plaza, the fans swirling the air around my fevered mind.

Later that afternoon, from a distance and unseen, I stood and watched.

Adam Berney was playing baseball with Kenny in the deserted parking lot. They had chalked a square, the pitching target—which served as home plate—on the wall of the empty factory. Kenny pitched, a lime green tennis ball, while Adam stood in for his swings.

I would never talk to my mother again. She was gone.

Standing there in the sun, beside the vacant lot in Ashland, Kentucky, in August, I now understood, was part of healing.

The skin would grow stronger, tougher, the world more focused on the present. I knew this from the experience of the stillbirth. There had been a year of grief and coping before I had functioned adequately. By then, Fran and I had ceased to have meaning as a couple and could not recapture our former lives. Everything had changed. And the new skin, although it looked the same, was always sore to the touch.

Squinting against the brightness, I watched the pitch, the swing, the miss.

My son, if he had lived, would be about their age.

All day, I thought. They can do this all day.

It must be wonderful.

2

AT 7:30 P.M., I WALKED UP THE FRONT STEPS OF THE PALE BLUE FRAME house and rang the top buzzer. Within seconds, Jeanne opened the door and stepped out, closing it behind her. She wore a summery cotton top and a white skirt. Her eyes, I noticed, had liner on them, and she was wearing lipstick. And she was wearing perfume, a subtle, Southern scent.

"You look great."

"Thanks."

"Hope I'm not underdressed." I looked down at myself, holding my hands palm outward.

"You look like a million bucks."

We started down the steps. "Do we need a car? I've got one."

She shook her head. "We can walk. It's close."

"Feels like rain."

"Not for a while," she said. "For a while, it'll just be hot and the wind'll blow." She looked at me. "Maybe in the night."

"You're the expert."

She put her arm through mine as we walked, and it felt like it belonged.

The Chimney Corner Tea Room was on Carter near 15th, and did indeed look pleasant—more like a cottage than a restaurant. The view from our table through the front window was colored by an array of purple flowers outside that were as high as a hedge. It was a family restaurant, and the better-off families of Ashland were about us, scrubbed clean in shirtsleeves and cotton dresses.

When I saw the prices on the menu, though, I spoke up. "This is a cut above McDonald's. I think this one should be on me, too." I tried to sound firm.

"Nonsense."

"Dutch treat, at least."

"*My* treat, Leo Nolan from Canada. Men your age are always tryin' to buy a woman, without even knowin' you're doin' it."

I was chastised. "I didn't mean—"

"I know you didn't. It's me has to get it straight in my head, too. Been too many years when I didn't get it myself. I'm asserting myself," she said, a blend of pride and coyness on her face. "Woman has to assert herself, clear the air."

I relaxed, smiling. "Man my age," I said.

"Is just the right age," she finished. "Just needs a little tunin', like a piano." She smiled. "Just a little."

I let her pick the wine.

In the corner of the restaurant sat a man in shirt and tie, wearing dark glasses, playing the electric organ and singing "Come Saturday Morning."

"He's blind." Jeanne didn't look at him as she said it. "Been here for years."

I nodded, not knowing what to say.

Jeanne ordered the seafood platter, and I decided to try the catfish, "a Kentucky specialty." "They just fry it in batter," she explained. "They do that to everything in Kentucky."

"Will they serve it with biscuits, too?"

"You bet."

I sipped the wine, a California white.

"How's your cholesterol level?" she asked.

"Haven't had it checked."

"Better book yourself in when you get back to Canada."

The blind organ player began singing "Mona Lisa."

She studied me for a long time in silence. Then she said: "You're a cop, right?"

"What?"

"A cop. A federal agent. What do they have up there in Canada? State troopers? Mounties?"

"Good Lord, Jeanne—"

"I've gone out with cops. They keep to themselves. Like you. And there's always pieces missing from their stories. It's 'cause they want something from you."

"I assure you, I am not a cop." I gave her the most sincere look I had.

She considered, took a sip from her wine. "Really?" she asked.

"I am just what you see, and what I said. Nothing more."

"What are you doin' in Ashland, then? Really. We don't get tourists, and if you're not here on business, I'm stumped."

I sat back, thinking. She was too observant to play games with, her company too good to lose so quickly. And the bouquet of her perfume, mixed with the warm air and California wine, made me want to share some intimacy. I think most men's brains often work in this simple way.

And she deserved as much of the story as any sane person could handle.

"My mother died in March."

Her face straightened. "Oh. I'm sorry."

"She had a brother whom she hadn't seen for years. Ashland was his last known address. I came to see if I could find him."

She relaxed. Finally, what I was saying rang true for her. "You found him?"

"No," I said. "Not really."

She waited.

"We haven't heard from him for fifty years."

She looked incredulous, yet said nothing.

"Gonna do a little more digging around, see what I can find out."

"Fifty years . . . Jeez . . . Is he here¿ Still¿"

I thought of last night and the night before. "I don't know," I said.

"See," said Jeanne, pointing to my catfish. "What'd I tell you¿"

I looked at it. "A Kentucky specialty." I checked the batter. "You were right."

"I love those words."

"Pardon¿"

" 'You were right.' They just might be a woman's favorites."
I smiled.

"In my case, it's 'cause I'm not right often enough. But when I am, it feels good."

"It feels good for everybody. You don't have to be a woman." I cut into the catfish.

The organ player was singing "Red Roses for a Blue Lady."

"Where do you live in Toronto¿" she asked.

"I've got an apartment, downtown. A one-bedroom."

"Any family there¿"

I chewed, thinking. "Lots, I guess," I said at last. "My father's still alive. He's eighty years old. And I've got two brothers and two sisters."

"Big family."

I nodded.

"They all still live in Toronto¿"

"My older brother lives in Sudbury with his family. That's about two hundred miles north of Toronto. The rest of them, though, yeah. Around the city, and in its suburbs." I sat back, looked at her. "What about you?" I asked. "I met your mom."

"And my dad's there, too. And I've got an older sister. Just the two of us."

"She live in Ashland?"

"In Cincinnati, with her husband and two kids. Got a nice house, beautiful family. Adam likes to visit. No doubt about it," she said.

I waited.

"She's the family success story."

We listened to the man in the dark glasses finish his song.

"What happened to Adam's father?" I asked.

She chewed quietly for a moment. "He was in Dayton, last I heard." She shrugged. "I guess he's still there."

"You divorced?"

"Never married. When I got pregnant, he just left."

I digested this before I spoke. "Does he ever see Adam?"

"Not once, far as I know. He doesn't send a postcard, a Christmas card, or a birthday card. And he's never paid a dime in support."

I felt uncomfortable even listening to this account of such epic uninterest. "Did you get a lawyer?"

She shook her head. "I didn't need a lawyer. Once he left, I realized that I didn't need him. I realized what he was. I can look after myself."

"But he should—"

"Leo Nolan from Canada, you surely don't get it, do you?"

I was quiet.

"It isn't about what people should or shouldn't do. It's about what they do or don't do. Why would I want anything from him if he don't want his own son?" She stared at me, pushed herself back. "We got a homey little sayin' for a fella like him down here." There was a glint of steel in her eye that accompanied the half smile. "We say that he can go fuck himself."

I nodded slowly, sagely. "You know," I said. "We got that same homey sayin' up north."

"So what do you think of the music?" I asked.

The blind organist was doing his rendition of "My Way."

"I'm not too crazy about any music by anyone who didn't die violently in a motorized vehicle. You know what I mean?"

"Buddy Holly," I said.

She nodded. "Him and others. That's the idea."

"You like some more wine?" I held out the bottle.

"You bet." She held out her glass.

We stood outside the pale blue frame house. Even in the dark, the wind was blowing warm and sultry.

"No rain yet?" I asked.

Jeanne shook her head. "Just the wind, for a while. Then'll come the lightning. It'll come in sheets from the east and the north. Afterward, there'll be rain. Lots of it."

I kissed her. It was the right thing to do, because it came to me spontaneously.

When I stepped back, she looked at me fondly. "Last time, we shook hands."

"Don't know what got into me," I said.

"It's only after nine o'clock."

I waited.

"You like to come upstairs for a while?"

"Very much." Then I pondered. "What about Adam?"

"I can get him around midnight. Mom won't mind. Girl doesn't get too many nice dates she can afford to mess up when she gets to my age."

"That's a couple of hours from now." I looked about me, at the lights in the windows of surrounding houses, wondered who was sitting out on their front verandas. "What'll the neighbors say?"

"We got a homey little sayin' about that down here."

"I'll bet you do."

She took my hand and led me up the walk.

3

WE MADE LOVE THAT NIGHT

With the warm night wind sweeping across the Appalachians, up the winding Ohio, and through the open second-story windows of the robin's-egg house, we explored each other's bodies in the hesitant manner of all new lovers—careful, uncertain of the limits. And when it was over, it was as right and as comfortable as the dinner at the Chimney Corner Tea Room had been.

I have a memory of her outline in the darkened room, of the sway of the mattress, of the cool sheets wrapped about us, and of the taste of her mouth as the lightning flashed finally in the skies, as she had said it would. And, strangely, of all things, I remember the feel of her fingers as they trailed along my shoulders, and how much I needed that touch.

In the dimly lit room, I thought of Adam's father, walking away from this woman and his son. I thought of all the things I could never comprehend, and knew that they were just beginning.

At midnight, we walked to where my car was parked behind the Scott Hotel and drove to Carter Avenue. I waited while Jeanne went inside her parents' bungalow, and came out with a sleepyhead boy in tow, then drove them back to their home.

On the veranda, she opened the front door. "Upstairs," she said to him. "Into the bathroom. It's late. I'll be up in a minute."

She guided Adam through the door, closing it softly behind him.

When we were alone, I held her. "Ritchie Valens," I said.

"Pardon?"

"He sang 'Donna.' He was in the plane with Buddy Holly."

I felt her smile against my chest. Then: "I've got to go. Mom stuff," she added.

"I know."

"Look." She pointed over my shoulder.

I turned. Sheets of lightning, without sound, rippled the sky across the river. Watching the spectacle, this woman in my arms, I wondered where I was, how all this had happened.

"I'm not supposed to ask," she said. "But I will."

"What?"

"Will I see you again?"

I pulled her head back to my chest, where it fit snugly below my neck. "Yes," I breathed. "Yes." And I meant it.

But already I was alive with what would happen next that night.

The lightning flashed at my back, leaves on the trees stirring in the wind, and I knew, even then, that I was going to see him within an hour.

"Yes," I said.

I stood and waited.

He came out of the hospital at 1:00 A.M., as he had previously, and we replayed the entire walk along Lexington, 14th, the pause at the Scott, then onto Winchester. It had become a mantra, a ritual like the Mass, where each step in the ceremony was ordained, cherished, and respected.

When he stood, finally, across from the First Bank and Trust Company building, he put his hands in his pockets as I knew he would, turned and faced me, and once again, our eyes met.

And yes, there were sheets of silent lightning electrifying

the air as we stood there, and I have no idea whether it was pure coincidence or not. But it happened that way, and the images that I remember are burned into my brain as white-hot flashes and heart stops in the night, as the world turned inside out, and I shared a timeless point in the universe with my uncle, who was younger than I was.

I licked my lips before I spoke. "Jack¿" The word was a long-awaited, soft thunderclap.

He smiled, puzzled.

"Jack Radey¿"

He nodded. "Yes."

My heart flooded with a sudden ache. I forged ahead. "I'm a friend of Margaret's. A friend of your sister."

In the darkness, his eyes brightened. "Way down here¿ You're kidding!" He stepped forward, closing the space between us.

I remained frozen, light-headed.

His shirt was plain white, open at the neck—the collar from another era; his pants were flannel—too warm for either the time of year or the place—with double-pleated front. "Do you live here¿" he asked.

"No. I'm on vacation. Margaret knew I might get down here. She gave me your address. Asked me to look you up, make sure everything's all right."

He shook his head, smiling. His eyes were bright blue, like my mother's. "Good old Marg. Always keeping tabs on me. Watchin' out for little brother." He was both amused and pleased. Then his eyes met mine again. "I'm sorry—I didn't catch your name."

"Leo." He waited for a last name. When I didn't offer it, I added, "Just tell her Leo dropped by to see how you were, to see if there was any pressing news, next time you write."

He accepted that.

I walked toward him, closing the space between us. I saw

my shadow ahead of me, flickering wildly on the pavement, a transient fragment cast by the lightning with no sound. And as I neared him, as the distance was closed, the air became still, and the shadow disappeared.

It happened like that.

I held my breath, looked around.

We stood, face to face, in the silence, in the dark.

In the past.

8

Monday, October 8, 1934

EVERYTHING CHANGED.

The temperature had dropped slightly, the wind was gone, and the approaching storm had ceased to exist.

The streetlamps were dark, cast iron, with gracefully arched necks, their bulbs suspended downward. And in that soft light, I began to note the classic, hulking black coupés of the 1930s parked intermittently about the street. Then I turned and stared in the opposite direction, my eyes catching the announcement for *King Kong*, starring Fay Wray and Bruce Cabot, jutting over the sidewalk below the green marquee of the Paramount Theater, resplendent with its new golden lettering and trim.

I glanced in a window beside me—a clothing store—my eyes scanning the display of suits, coats, shoes: *Ayer's All-Wool Tweed Coat, $9.75, Delivered; Lady's High Fashion Dress, $2.98, Delivered; Black Calfskin or White Leather Pump, Featuring a Smart New Bow, $2.45 Pair, Delivered.*

I stood on Winchester Avenue, in Ashland, Kentucky, and let it happen.

* * * *

"Where you staying?" he asked.

I shrugged.

"You really on vacation?" There was a playfulness to his question. I thought of Jeanne. The story had an obvious timelessness to its incredibility.

"Sort of," I said.

"Yeah," he said. "Like everybody else." He took a package of cigarettes from his pants pocket, shook one loose, placed it between his lips, then held the package toward me.

"No. Thanks."

He smiled, put them away. He lit his own, inhaling the smoke, enjoying the luxury. Then he seemed to study me. "How'd you know it was me?"

"I've seen pictures," I lied. "Of Margaret and you."

He smiled again, his pleasure obvious. "Where do you know Marg from? I thought I knew all her friends."

"You've been gone for a while now."

He nodded. "That's true."

"Marg helped my family when we moved into the neighborhood." I began to amaze myself with my story. "Helped me look after my father. He's my family," I added, trying to flesh out the picture. I realized that I must look positively middle-aged to Jack.

"How's Tommy?" he asked, watching me.

"He's in good shape. Still working."

"And the kids?"

"Ronny and Anne?" I smiled. "Healthy as horses."

He relaxed even more. "So you live up around Yonge and Eglinton, do you?"

I nodded.

"Too far north of the city for my tastes. I guess I'm kind of a downtown kid."

He nodded in the direction of the railway lines, just this side of the river. "You sleeping down there?"

I followed his gaze and took my cue. "Isn't everybody?"

He seemed to consider. The cigarette smoke floated upward in the still air. "I'm not sure what you're doin', Leo, but any friend of Marg's a friend of mine. It's as simple as that." He gestured with his cigarette toward the railway yards. "Lots sleep down there. I know." He pondered. "Maybe I can help you."

I waited.

"I know a nice place. I think we can work something out."

I followed his glance. The Scott Hotel in its prime, even in the dark, was a very nice place.

We slipped into the Scott, up the stairs, and into room 8 on the third floor.

Jack's things were spread throughout the room. Mine were gone.

He pulled a pillow and blanket from the bed—the same white-painted iron bedstead that I had known—and tossed them on the floor by the window. "Good enough?" he asked.

"It'll do fine," I said. The furniture was new.

He nodded, smiled. "We'll talk in the morning."

I went over to the window, looked out. The church was still there. Then I sat down on the floor with my back against the wall, staring at him.

He smiled, dropped back onto the bed and ran his hands through his dark, curly hair, as I had seen him do before. "What?" he asked.

"How do you know you can trust me?" I frowned. "How do you know who I am?"

He continued to smile, that magic, disarming smile, his eyes burning with a belief in a future and things that I could not share. "Who are any of us?" He paused. "A hunch," he said.

"I play hunches. Can't help myself. Marg always said I was a little naïve." Another shrug. "What can you do?"

I was quiet, listening to my heart beat, listening to the silence of the years breaking open.

"And you're a friend of Marg's. It's enough." He seemed content, pulled off a shoe and leaned back on his elbow, gazing at me. "You must know that she makes everyone a better person just because she believes in them." His eyes twinkled. "You know what I mean?"

"Yes," I said.

It was true.

"In the morning," he said.

I listened.

"We'll talk."

He turned off the light. In the darkness, I could see the tip of his cigarette flare when he inhaled, smell its smoke as it wended its way out the window by my side.

When it was dashed out, I must have slept.

Or dreamed that I slept.

I woke with the sunlight streaming in above me. I was still on the floor, Jack was still in the bed.

He pushed up on to an elbow when he heard me stir and smiled.

I touched the wall beside me. It was solid. It was real.

I looked for my car at the back of the Scott when we were outside. It was gone.

"Where we going?" I asked. He went ahead of me across Winchester Avenue.

"Get something to eat."

"Where?" We reached the other side and stopped.

"Soup kitchen." He looked at me. "Unless you got some money."

I reached into my pants pocket and took out my wallet. I opened it and looked in.

It was empty.

We sat at a plank table in a warehouse near the east end of town. Dozens of men, at similar tables, surrounded us. The room was lit by bare light bulbs, hanging from wiring strung over thick, wooden rafters.

With a twisted fork and knife in my hands, I stared at the rough metal plate.

Jack was eating. He caught me studying the food in front of me, sat back and watched. Then he said, "Never eat in one of these places before?"

I shook my head. "No."

He continued chewing, thinking. "You got no money, you'll get used to it."

There was little conversation anywhere about us. The sounds of metal against metal pervaded in its stead.

Everyone had the same meal: white beans boiled in water, two slices of dry bread, and a cup of tea.

I sampled the beans. They were almost completely taste-less. "Is it always the same food?"

Jack nodded as he ate. "Mostly." He swallowed. "Some-times you get porridge in the morning. Not too often, though."

"Three times a day?"

"Twice. At ten and five."

The tea was bitter.

He smiled. "Once, though, local guy shot a bear. Donated it. Everybody had diarrhea for forty-eight hours." He shrugged. "Poor bloody bear," he said.

Two gaunt, sallow men sat at the same bench as us, shoveling the food into their mouths. Their clothes smelled like the no-torious Saint Clair West area in Toronto—the area dominated by the Canada Packers meat processing plant. When they left, I met Jack's eyes. "They work in an abattoir or something?"

He shook his head, sipped his tea. "Least they were clean," he said. "I got some store-bought soap back at the hotel. Makes things nice. But I've done what they've done. Mixed pork fat, wood ashes, and salt. It makes a kind of soap. It works. But," he said, "it takes a lot of sun-baking to get the smell out of your clothes." He shrugged. "Sometimes you got no choice."

Around noon, we walked in the hot sun through the railway yards by the river. On the far side of the tracks, we stood high up over the Ohio—in the place where I had been by myself, in whatever other life that had been—looking down on the stony strand. Smoke drifted up through the leaves of a sycamore tree from three different campfires. A dozen or so men idled about.

"Ridin' the rods," he said. "Is that how you got here?"

I thought of the car that no longer existed. "No," I said. "Hitched."

He lit a cigarette, inhaled deeply. "You're lucky. Hard to get rides." The smoke drifted from his mouth and nose into the sunshine. "But maybe you're good at it. Some are better at it than others. Same as this." He nodded in the direction of the men below. "They say it takes about a thousand miles before you get real good at it. Get to know where the trains slow, get to know the whistles, the lights, the bells. Get to know a local from an express. Get your timing down, so's you can grab a moving ladder or jump at the right time when you want off."

We stood, squinting, watching them.

"Do the local police bother them?"

He looked at me, mildly surprised, then smiled. "Keep 'em moving, that's their motto. If they arrest them as vagrants, it costs a dollar a day to keep 'em." He stared down at them. "Even the police don't want 'em."

I watched the trail of the campfires' smoke, adrift in the afternoon haze. "What are they cooking?"

Jack shrugged. "Gophers, squirrels, possums. Whatever they can catch."

I was quiet.

"Maybe weeds or dandelions in a soup."

I didn't know what to say.

"Could be worse."

I looked at him.

"Could be a bear."

He grinned boyishly. But in his eyes I saw something I tried to put my finger on, something that eluded description.

I think it was sadness.

Later that afternoon we sat on the porch swing on the front veranda of the Scott Hotel.

"You're doing okay, though, aren't you, Jack? Got a job. Place to live. Why eat in the soup kitchens?"

He grimaced, bared his teeth, which were a startling white, while he reflected. Then he said: "I got nothing. Job barely keeps me alive. Eating there most of the time is a way of stayin' even." He paused. "I treat myself, sometimes. A meal. A hot dog from a restaurant. A movie. Cigarettes. But not much. Not too much." His eyes were crinkled at the corners from the glare, from thinking. From the truth.

I saw the Paramount marquee for *King Kong* again, and recalled the letter of September 30 that my father had read over the phone. "What's today's date?" I asked.

"It's the eighth."

"Of October."

He nodded.

I gestured toward the theater. "You seen that one yet?"

"Saw it the other night."

I fell quiet.

"Sad," he said. "The ape gets a raw deal."

"Margaret read me some of your letters."

He looked at me with a combination of bemusement and surprise.

"She thinks you're doing okay. Mentioned a car, clothes, job as a photographer with a Detroit firm."

He bowed his head, smiling meekly.

I watched him. "It's not true, is it?"

He looked me in the eye. "No," he said. The word was very soft.

I nodded, understanding.

We were both quiet for a long time.

"Some people still live real good," he said. "Bankers. Lawyers. The ones that feed on the rest. Inherited money. You know."

I put my hands in my pockets, leaned my head back and stared into the endless blue sky.

"But it's like a giant iceberg. Just the tip is showin'. Most of it's just gliding along, out of sight, massive." He paused. "Dangerous."

He said the last word carefully, nodding to himself, then lit a cigarette.

The screen door swung open and a young man of about thirty strode out. "Jack," he said. "How you doin'?" He put his hands on his hips.

Jack greeted him with a smile, a nod. "Good," he said.

The newcomer was about five-nine, strongly built, the arms showing from his T-shirt well muscled and tanned. His hair was sandy blond, slicked back straight. He glanced at me, his eyes narrowing.

Jack picked up the cue. "Leo." He touched my arm. "Like you to meet someone."

I stood up, staring inquisitively at the man.

"This is the man who owns the hotel—"

I saw who he was in that moment, the same moment that I heard his name.

"—Stanley Matusik."

I saw the lined toughness that was to come, the tufts of white hair that would be left, and as he extended his hand toward me, the future calluses on his eighty-year-old skin just beginning.

He squeezed my hand warmly. "Pleased to meet you."

"My pleasure," I managed to say, unable to take my eyes from him.

His hand, like his body, was strong. For in him, there was still hope, a world of infinite possibility.

There was still the future.

"Leo's from Toronto," said Jack.

Stanley's eyebrows rose. "Really?"

"Friend of my sister."

"You come down through Toledo?" he asked.

"Yeah," I said, thinking. "I did."

He let go my hand. "Big trouble there earlier this year. You see any of it?"

"I heard about it. You keep your ears open, you hear about lots."

Stanley smiled. Then he turned to Jack. "Jack was there."

Jack didn't meet his gaze.

"Big eye-opener for him."

"I'll bet. Big eye-opener for everybody."

"Get him to tell you about it sometime."

I looked at Jack, who was still in his own thoughts. "I will," I said. "Sometime."

Jack looked at me, from far off.

"You workin', Leo?" Stanley Matusik asked.

"No," I said. "I'm not." I went with the simplest answer.

"Figures," he said.

We listened.

"Wasn't for Teresa's parents, we wouldn't have nothin' either. They set us up with this place. Cost them their restaurant last year." He paused. " 'Cause they're good people, they don't complain too much about it. Took care of their own. They say that's the best anyone can do in this life."

I let my eyes stray along the front wall of the building, recalling another conversation with Stanley, about how his in-laws had loaned them the down payment.

"Teresa works at Woolworth's."

He had told me this, of course, but with its retelling came the flash and memory of my own life, of Jeanne, of her touch.

"Makes eleven dollars a week. Rockefeller paid six million in tax alone. Somethin's definitely screwed up, wouldn't you say?"

It didn't need an answer.

"Willys plant in Toledo dropped from twenty-eight thousand workers to four thousand. Hung on for a while that way. Then went bust. Unemployment in Cincinnati's over twenty percent. And another twenty percent is employed only part-time. More'n a thousand homes a day in this country are bein' taken over by mortgage holders." He looked at me and half smiled. "I guess you could say that it all obsesses me." He nodded. "Yes, indeed," he said, "you could surely say that."

Jack spoke. "Tell him about your dad."

I glanced at him, saw my uncle's blue eyes sparkling with intensity.

It was a prompt that Stanley heeded. "Died in thirty-two. Tuberculosis. Was a coal miner, Harlan County. In thirty-one, he was asked to dig for thirty-three cents a ton, so like everybody else, he joined the union. Mine blacklisted all the men, and their own company doctor wouldn't treat the families. My little sister, age seven, died of pneumonia that year. My dad died the next. They drove the miners to starvation. Was as simple as that. My mom was a midwife. She saw forty-three babies die in her arms that winter. Hunger. Sickness. You name it. She told me one time that some of them died with their little stomachs literally bust open." His face had hardened. "So, yeah, I think it's fair to say that it all obsesses me." He inhaled and exhaled slowly, regaining composure. "Fair indeed."

I looked at Jack's face, saw the hypnotic effect the tale had on him, thought of his experience as strikebreaker in Toledo, felt him straddling that imaginary line, fists clenched, and saw him leaning now, with quiet passion, toward Stanley Matusik.

Stanley's eyes focused on the two men coming up the street. Then he looked at me. "Got some things to tend to." He shook my hand again. "Nice meetin' you, Leo." He looked at Jack. "If Jack thinks you're a good man, maybe we can talk some more. Some of us got plans, haven't we, Jack?"

"You bet."

Stanley looked at the sky. "Gonna rain next few days. Can feel it." His face wrinkled. "Not good. Not good at all."

I didn't understand why the rain was so bad. But I didn't ask.

I'd understand soon enough.

He put his hands on his hips. "Comin' across the Appalachians, from the east."

I heard the echo of Jeanne's voice.

He looked back at Jack. "All our troubles seem to come from the east." Then he smiled and looked at me. "Leo," he said. "Ashland's the last damn place somebody from Canada ought to be comin' to to better himself."

"You could be right," I said, having thought the same thing myself.

He looked at Jack again, twitched his head, smiling wryly. "But you never know, do you, buddy?"

"Never," said Jack. And he smiled that startling, white smile.

"Afternoon, Stan. Jack." The two men in overalls and work boots nodded abruptly to us, then proceeded inside the Scott Hotel. Jack and Stanley's eyes flicked momentarily to one another, then dropped.

A moment later, I found them studying me.

Through the screen door, I could hear the fading footsteps of the two men as they descended stairs into the basement.

Stanley broke the silence. "Gotta go." He reached out his hand again. "Nice meetin' you, Leo."

I shook it.

"Talk to you later, Jack." He looked at me. "Maybe you, too."

"Hope so," I said.

He turned and went inside, following the men downstairs.

I followed Jack into the Woolworth's on Winchester where Jeanne worked, the place new and shiny.

Jeanne wasn't there.

My eyes scanned glass jars of Baby Ruth bars, cookies, and stick candy as we strode through the aisles. A BB air rifle was 79¢. A leather basketball, a dollar. And I stopped for a second to touch a baseball glove, with the ball, sold as a package for $1.25, thinking of Jeanne and Adam.

I saw silk ties for 55¢, shirts for 47¢, a pullover sweater for $1.95. Toothpaste was a quarter, a linen tablecloth a dollar. And cigarettes were 15¢.

We sat at the dinette counter, on the red-and-chrome swivel chairs, and I stared unabashedly at the sight of an achingly pretty young Teresa Matusik, who materialized suddenly amid the collage of signs and prices and soda treats arrayed behind her.

Her hair, I thought, was beautiful.

I looked at Jack, then back at her.

And I remembered that it had been done in a beauty parlor.

"Leo, this is Teresa."

She wiped her hand on the white apron, then placed it in mine. "Pleased to meet you."

I found my voice. "Hi, Teresa." I tried, rather unsuccessfully, not to stare.

Her face crinkled. "Not from around here, are you?"

I shook my head. "Toronto. Like Jack."

"Can tell from your accent. North somewhere."

"Leo's a friend of my sister Marg. Might stay a bit."

"Ah." She seemed to understand something. What it was, I wasn't sure.

"Depends," I said.

"Do you think Barbara could spare us a sandwich?" asked Jack. "Keep body and soul together?"

She smiled at him. "See what she can do." She moved off down the counter.

When she was rummaging in a loaf of white bread, I asked, "Who's Barbara?"

He grinned. "Hutton. Woolworth heiress. Poor little rich girl. Who else?" He turned to me, speaking under his breath. "I figure Barbara can afford to treat me to the occasional sandwich. You, too. Nobody's hurt." He glanced down the counter, smiling that startling smile at Teresa, who smiled back. "Only reason I come here," he said.

His last sentence settled like a door clicking solidly shut. Yet glancing from one to the other of them, watching what passed between them, I saw, with wonder and trepidation, that there was clearly another reason why he came here.

* * * *

That night, Jack went to work at the hospital and left me alone in his room. I sat in a chair by the open window and watched the sheets of lightning flash across my surreal world, knowing that this was all leading somewhere, through the past, through the future. Finally, I began to hear the rolls of distant thunder, and knew that the rain, which seemed spread across fifty years, was coming at last.

But it wasn't until some time after midnight, while I was still sitting in the chair, between waking and dreaming, between action and possibility, that the noises coming from the basement began to infiltrate my consciousness.

I listened.

Opening the door, I stood on the third-floor landing.

Muffled voices. A pause. Hammering.

Silence.

I descended the stairs. As on the journey into the past, through lightning and heat, I was being drawn down, led beneath the apparent schematics of things, into the subterranean world of some dark truth.

9

Tuesday, October 9, 1934

THE MIND IS PLATED WITH ELECTRICALLY GALVANIZED IMAGES. THERE are incidents, voices, that never leave us, and we replay them at odd moments, letting them speak to us with their eerie clarity. The past is a scrapbook of clipped dialogues and scenes, of which childhood is a part.

I have a memory of my mother sitting in the aluminum-and-cloth folding chair on the front veranda of the house in which my father still lives today. It is summer. I am eight, perhaps ten years of age. I ask my mother if she could have anything she wants, what would she have.

Peace and quiet, she says.

I do not understand this, so I try again. No, really, what would you have?

Suddenly, she confides in me, a child, the fourth of her five. I'd like to know, she says, what happened to my brother Jack. I'd like to know what became of him, why he never wrote again.

My mother has told me stories about herself and her brother growing up. I know his name. I have a picture of him in my head, based on a faint memory of a photograph I once saw. Even in my innocence, though, I realize that I have elicited a truth that may have surprised both of us.

Why, I ask, do you think you haven't heard from him? What happened to him?

She is quiet.

The summer is quiet.

Childhood stands still.

I think he must be dead, she says finally. I don't think there could be any other reason. Otherwise, she says, he'd have written.

The film in my head runs out at this point, and I cannot see or hear any more.

But I remember the feeling of being allowed into this secret place. I remember it as one of the closest moments I ever had with my mother.

On the second-floor landing, I stood and listened again. Voices, quiet, then voices. Hammering. Quiet.

I waited another minute. A bit of soft laughter rolled up the stairs, then more talking.

The sound of a shovel scraping dirt from a cement surface. In Ashland, Kentucky.

I continued downward, feeling the tide rising to meet me.

The first time I ever saw my mother cry I was three years old. She was in the kitchen, and Nanny, my grandmother, my father's mother, was comforting her, holding her, letting her cry on her shoulder.

I hadn't known that mothers cried until then.

The film in my head begins with that image.

What's wrong? I ask.

No one pays attention.

What's the matter?

Go upstairs, Nanny tells me. Away you go.

I head onto the stairs, where I sit, halfway up, listening, looking through the rails. My mother is still crying. I don't understand it. I am scared.

Later, Nanny tells me that my mother's father died. I try to understand how sad she must have been to cry like that.

No one took me to the funeral home or to the service.

I have no memory of him.

On the stairs, I thought. I am still on the stairs. Going down, instead of up. Jack, I thought. Jack. Are you down there?

I do not pray anymore. I cannot believe as I once did. Everything changed.

I am forty. It is a gray area, a crossroads. I approach a world without the past, my parents disappearing, one at a time, slowly, in bits. The people about me, friends, brothers, sisters, are changing into whatever it is they will become next. Their own children are growing up.

We had a name picked out for my stillborn son. It is a name we never spoke aloud afterward. But I use it when I speak to him in my head, when I try to explain to him what happened. You see, he was alive. Once. I know he was. I felt him move and kick, often, before he was born.

He knows his name. It is Aidan.

I never say it out loud.

It hadn't occurred to me that my concept of a basement was formed by my experience as a Canadian, or as one from the northern states of fifty years hence—an area carved out neatly and fashioned to harbor the mechanics of a house: furnace, electricity, plumbing, storage. And then you could opt for finishing it, adding an entire living level.

I reached the bottom of the stairs, below the main floor, and found myself standing in mud. No furnace. Nothing but light bulbs dangling intermittently from an electric wire that dwindled away into the darkness.

I could smell the earth around me, damp and primitive. Focusing my eyes, I looked about and saw a large room that was the size of what a full basement might be, a cave beneath the Scott Hotel, filled with enormous piles of moist brown subsoil.

And I could hear men digging.

Maybe nature constructs us in such a way that we are destined to be only what we can be, what we were always meant to be. Experience then tests us. It is only when we have survived the crucibles that we start to find out what we hold true and valuable, who we are. Our spirit discovers how much it can absorb.

I think of white-hot metal hammered relentlessly. Then we cool, bubble in water, hissing in pain and wonder, and what emerges is truer, harder, purer.

The shadows fall away.

We glow, ready again.

The string of light bulbs led to the far side of the room, toward the sounds that echoed, feebly, all the way to the third floor. Shading my eyes from the glare with my hand, I stepped, carefully, slowly, through the mud and earth, following the lights to the far end of the room.

And stared in silence at the tunnel that had been dug in the wall in front of me, at the lights snaking out into the subterranean channel beneath the streets of Ashland.

Two-by-fours and two-by-sixes blocked off an opening six feet in height by four feet in width. Tram tracks disappeared down the center of the tunnel.

In my head, I heard Stanley's voice. Was a coal miner, Harlan County. In thirty-one, he was asked to dig for thirty-three cents a ton.

I stepped onto the ties and entered the tunnel, walking slowly, carefully. I seemed to be heading east, out under the street. About twenty feet into the tunnel, the noises of men working becoming clearer, closer, it all hit me with a brazen clarity, like the tumblers in a giant lock sliding open.

Bank's a bank . . . , he had said. But that one . . . That one's still there.

I stood for several minutes watching them dig before anyone noticed me: the two men that I had seen entering the hotel earlier, Stanley, two others whom I did not know.

And Jack.

The air was scarcely breathable—close, humid, fetid. The men were naked to the waist, crowded together in the confines of the tunnel, covered in sweat and dirt, ankle-deep in mud.

Slowly, one by one, they straightened, stopped what they were doing, stared at me, brows wrinkled, mouths set. The two strangers at the far dirt-face leaned on their shovels. Stanley let his pickaxe settle at his feet. The two men I had met earlier held their shovels in front of them, tools that had shape-shifted into weapons, their knuckles showing white.

Finally, Jack turned and met my gaze. He rested one hand on the small tram filled with freshly dug earth. Even in the harsh dimness of a single light bulb, his body streaked with grime, surrounded by puddles, mud, crow bars, I saw his blue eyes flash recklessly.

They flashed, I saw, like sun on a waterfall, the river full of rapids, running deep into underground caverns.

They waited in silence. Their glances flickered to the empty spaces behind me, to where the tunnel dwindled into a string of harsh light-bulb pearls.

Waiting.

Jack spoke first. "This here's Leo."

They still waited, listened.

I answered their unspoken question. "I'm alone," I said.

The two leaning on their shovels shifted their weight.

"I thought I heard something. I came to see." I shrugged.

"What do you see?" asked Stanley. His voice was soft.

They were motionless.

I looked at them. I looked from one to the next, each in turn, mud-stained and still as stopped clocks. I felt the rapids cascading from Jack's eyes flow into my chest with a soundless tumult. "Dreams," I said. Then I breathed slowly, in and out, my heart beating like a bird's wings. "I see dreams."

"He might not be alone." One of the strangers spoke.

They squinted around me, listened.

"You alone, Leo?" Jack asked.

I nodded. "Yes."

Jack looked at me. Then he turned around and spoke to the stranger. "I think he's alone."

"He ain't from around here. He talks funny," the man continued.

"He talks funny like me," Jack said.

"I'm a friend of Jack's sister," I said.

Jack smiled.

I watched them. I listened to the silence below the earth. I listened to my heart. Then I spoke again. "I can help," I said.

Jack nodded. The white teeth showed as the smile broadened, and I saw my mother's face.

The rapids thundered in my veins. "I want to help."

We stood in the mud in the basement back under the Scott Hotel. They seemed satisfied that I was alone.

"This here's Emmett and Henry." Stanley introduced me to

the two men who had passed me on the front verandah the previous afternoon.

They were sturdy, strong men, in their early thirties I guessed, whose hands, I could see, bore the calluses of hard work.

"And George and Jimmy."

George was round-faced and perhaps the oldest of the group—maybe forty. Jimmy's red hair was matted and filthy. Irish, I thought.

George looked at Stanley. "I dunno about this."

Stanley's eyes crinkled. He looked at Jack, then back at me. He dropped his head, thinking.

"Don't want to make a mistake," said Jimmy. His feet shifted uneasily.

"What are our choices?" Stan asked.

They were silent.

"C'mon. What are they?"

Nobody answered.

"Pretty quiet bunch. You know what they are. Same's I do." He placed his hands on his hips. "Leo's either in or he's out." He looked at me. "Aren't you, Leo? If you're out, could be dangerous to us all."

I scanned their faces. They looked scared. And because they were scared, they might be dangerous. But that was not a real factor in my decision. Their fear was a deeply rooted human fear, different from the fear of someone caught in an act of wrongdoing. I felt that what they feared was not me.

"I'd like to be in. I can help."

Again, nobody spoke. I glanced at Jack. There was the faint trace of smile left on his face.

Stanley paused. Then he said: "Believin' a man is a tricky business. Man says one thing, does another. Happens all the time. 'Specially when he's scared."

I looked at Jack, Stanley, Jimmy. "I'm not scared."

"Maybe you should be," George said. His fingers gripped his shovel tightly.

"Maybe." I had no idea what I was doing here, how I had even gotten here.

I looked again at Jack, felt his excitement, felt more alive that I had in years. Below the ground in Ashland, I had discovered six men digging for a future, with hope and craziness and desperation.

And I was in awe of them all.

"I'll vouch for him."

They all turned to stare at Jack.

"He's just a guy. He knows my sister, back home."

The others listened to him.

"He's okay," he said. And then the smile came back in full bloom. "I can just tell. Somehow."

"He could be a cop, a Fed, Pinkerton," George said.

Jack smiled. "Nah," he said. Then even he looked a bit perplexed. "Any guy who could find me way he did, with nothin' but scraps of letters to recall and old photographs way back in his head, it's kinda like he's meant to be here, with us."

Stanley looked at Jack. "Hope you're right," he said at last.

Jack nodded. "I am," he said.

"You know what's goin' on?" Stanley asked.

I nodded.

They said nothing, waiting for me to tell them. Emmett reached for a water bottle, took a long swig from it, then passed it to Henry.

"Jobs dried up and blew away," I said.

They listened.

"Two million men roaming the country looking for jobs, handouts. Maybe three million. Maybe more."

Henry passed the water bottle to George.

"More'n twenty million unemployed."

Jimmy nodded.

"And out there, right in the middle of it all, sits that big bank, fat with money."

They stared at me.

"And here you are, fellows who know a thing or two about diggin' tunnels, about goin' into the earth for what's there."

The bottle passed to Jack. He had it to his lips when I said, "I know about Toledo."

He stopped, lowered the bottle.

The men in the dank underworld studied him. Jack looked both bewildered and sheepish.

I shrugged. "We all learn. It's okay."

Jack didn't look at me.

"Who's right, who's wrong . . . What to do . . . Sometimes it isn't so clear . . ." I thought of my own life, of things that I didn't want to discuss, decisions I had made, things that embarrassed me when I remembered them.

Jack looked up, his face puzzled.

I stared hard at Stanley Matusik. "Who'll be hurt? Anybody in town? Neighbors?"

"No," he said. "We ain't gonna drill safety deposit boxes. Nothin' personal like that. Just cash. All insured. Nobody'll be hurt."

I nodded. It was madness. All of it. The idea. The tunnel. The Scott Hotel. My presence here.

All of it.

"I'm in," I said.

Stanley smiled.

Jack looked at me in wonder.

George was sitting on an overturned orange crate in the middle of the mud. "I once walked twenty-five miles looking for a job. Made it all the way to Portsmouth. Stopped at every store, every house, knocked and asked. Mostly, nobody'd talk to me." He shook his head. "Had to hitch home. Lost twelve pounds. Gettin' too old."

"Back in thirty-two," said Henry, "I was with a crowd of folks in Charleston. Men and women. We raided a grocery store near City Hall. We was all arrested. Twenty-six of us."

"My little boy died," said Emmett. "Scarlet fever." His lips moved, but nothing else came out. He fell silent.

"Somethin's wrong," said George, frowning. "Something's bad wrong."

"Money'll come in Friday, the twelfth. Bank'll be full all weekend. Leaves on the Monday. It's the same every month. We seen it, like clockwork," Stanley said.

"I'm not following."

"Comes in by train," he explained patiently, "from Huntington, Charleston, Bluefield, Roanoke. Stays the weekend. Goes on down to Lexington, Louisville. Ends up in Cincinnati, in a big goddamn bank. Bigger'n this one."

"How much?"

Stanley shrugged. "Depends. We got folks tell us some months it gets as high as four hundred thousand. Others, bad months, two-fifty, maybe three."

"Whose money is it?"

Jack smiled. He looked at Stanley.

"Barbara's," Stanley said.

I know my lips parted because I found myself closing them quickly.

"Barbara Hutton. Woolworth heiress."

I pictured Jeanne, then Teresa, behind the counter.

"Poor little rich girl," he said.

"She's got more stores than you or I got hairs on our head," said Stanley. "There's a Woolworth's in every town in America. Some got two, three of 'em. Ashland's got five."

"More'n a thousand throughout the country." Jimmy wiped his hand across his brow as he spoke, streaking the dirt. "Even up there in Canada, I hear," he said, looking at me closely.

I remembered the one at Yonge and Eglinton. I remembered the one at Queen and Yonge. Carlton and Yonge. The Danforth.

"Newspapers say she inherited forty-five million dollars," George said.

"I heard sixty-five million," said Emmett.

I looked at Jack. "She won't miss it," he said. "Nobody's hurt." Then he added, meeting my eyes: "Ain't like Toledo."

"Is this it?" I asked. "How many are in on this?"

"There are others," said Stanley. "They give us information, tools, lumber." He was silent for a moment. "You don't need to know, Leo."

I looked into the tunnel. It went in sixty, eighty, a hundred feet. I couldn't tell. "How close are you?"

"We'll be there by the fourteenth," said Stanley. He stepped in front of me. "We could use another strong back, just to be sure."

"This is crazy," I said. "You'll never do it. It's too much digging. Too far."

"My daddy was part of a crew cut a tunnel ten miles long one way, then twenty-three miles t'other," said Stanley. "Had to get 'round a ridge. He traveled 'bout five miles a day on his knees."

I studied the firm set of their faces again.

Crazy, I thought, completely exhilarated.

Then my head was dizzy with other faces: my mother, my father, my grandfather, Nanny, Jack Radey, my brothers and sisters. Jeanne and Adam.

Aidan.

10

Wednesday, October 10, 1934

THE NEXT MORNING, STANLEY, JACK AND I SIPPED COFFEE ON THE veranda of the Scott Hotel. It was only eight o'clock, but the sun was already warming.

"You know much about Barbara¿" Stanley asked.

"Some. Not much," I said.

"She got the inheritance last November. 'Bout a year ago."

"You read about her comin'-out party¿" asked Jack.

"Don't remember," I said.

"When she was eighteen." He thought for a moment. "Would be nineteen thirty. Was in all the papers and magazines."

I shrugged, smiled.

"Was at the Ritz-Carlton in New York. A thousand guests. Maurice Chevalier, Rudy Vallee, three other orchestras."

"For her, there weren't no Prohibition or Depression," said Stanley. "Was thousands of bottles of champagne, the papers said."

I began to realize the degree of people's obsession with her as I listened.

"Had flowers and trees flown in special from both coasts."

"Eucalyptus trees, from California," said Jack.

I had read once how farmers there during the Depression planted mile-long windbreaks of eucalyptus to keep the plowed topsoil from blowing away.

"One night only," said Stanley, emphasizing the point with his index finger. "Party for a little girl. Cost fifty thousand dollars."

"Two hundred fifty million dollars in sales in nineteen thirty-two for the company," Jack said. "She got married last year. Wore jewelry worth one million dollars. They say her lace lingerie for her weddin' night was made by a dozen nuns. Cost twenty thousand dollars."

"Speedboats, Argentinean polo ponies, the White Russian choir, European honeymoon," added Stanley. He paused. "All we wanted was union wages."

"Nobody'll be hurt," said Jack, his blue eyes sparkling, a missionary zeal spreading across his face. And he smiled that smile. "Drop in the bucket," he said.

"Only problem we might run into is rain," said Stanley.

I looked at him, listened.

"Rain and tunnels, they don't mix. Get a lot of it, could weaken the ground. Too much of it, could flood." He sipped his coffee, thought for a minute. "Been lots of flooding in this town. People in Ashland still talk about the big one of nineteen thirteen." He nodded toward the north. "River rose up. Happened in eighteen eighty-four, too, they say. Whole town went underwater two or three feet."

We all looked into the east, looked at the sky.

Later that evening, I dug with them, in the mud beneath the streets of Ashland. The shovel in my hands was real, but the sensation of being beneath the earth, buried treasure and Rosetta Stone lying in wait somewhere ahead of us, was not.

"My little girl, Jenny, she got typhoid last year," said Henry. "All her hair fell out. She's just turned eight years old this summer. Went through the school year bald-headed." He wheezed a load of dirt to one side. "Couldn't afford no wig for her. Leastways, no wig worth wearin'. Place in Louisville wanted fifty dollars for one made of human hair—blond, like her own." He paused, straightened, thinking. "Can't remember the last time I had fifty dollars all at one time." He placed his hand on the small of his back, working the muscles there with his fingers. He continued to think. "Don't think I ever had fifty dollars all at one time."

I straightened beside him.

"She got used to it," he said. "We all did."

There in the tunnel, the sound of men working about me, another filament of memory dangled down from my childhood. There had been a sidewalk construction pit a block or so from where I grew up—a hole at the southwest corner of Duplex and Eglinton. I was eight . . . perhaps ten years old . . . I watched them work, saw how the tunnel some twenty or thirty feet down went out under the street.

I have no idea what it was all for.

I went back after dinner, in the early evening, when everyone had gone home. Red flare lanterns had been placed around its perimeter, and it had been covered over with long construction planks. I played about it for quite a while, peering down between the planks, trying to see the mysteries below. At some point I realized that there was a ladder below the planks, and assuring myself that no one was about, I pulled one of the boards aside, boldly lifted one of the red lanterns, and descended into the pit.

To this day, I have no idea what made me do such a rash thing.

Alone, I explored far out under Eglinton Avenue. No one

knew I was there. Had there been an accident or cave-in, it would have been days perhaps before anyone discovered me.

It seems like madness to me now.

I played down there for about an hour. When I got home, my mother was frantic—a combination of maternal anger and fear.

Where were you? I was asked.

Playing, I answered.

Where?

Around the block on Duplex Avenue, I answered.

I was not allowed to cross the street.

No, you weren't . . . I've been around the block twice looking for you! Where were you? Where did you get all the mud on your shoes?

I couldn't answer.

I never told.

I knew, even then, that what I had done was foolish. I knew I would be in trouble. And I had not the guile to construct a more intricate story.

My mother's eyes were wild, and she was breathing heavily. She didn't believe me.

But I was back. That was enough. Her relief overcame all else.

We let it drop. Neither of us ever mentioned it again. Perhaps she forgot about it. I never did. My cave has been my secret ever since.

Just as everyone's childhood is such a secret.

I still remember the smell of the earth.

The earth below Ashland was soft and wet.

The tunnel cut through occasional springs, which ran into puddles that needed to be channeled back into a pit in the basement of the hotel. The pit was only a few feet deeper than the basement floor, and the sound of water running into it, into the pool at the bottom, was something that became a constant.

If one dug too low, Henry told me, one would inevitably meet the Ohio River. It was always there, he said. Just beneath us.

11

Thursday, October 11, 1934

I SLEPT UNTIL NOON. WHEN I WOKE, THE STIFFNESS OF THE MUSCLES in my back, arms, legs all told me what I already knew—that I had done more than I should have.

Jack was gone.

Gazing at the window ledge above me, I touched the wall beside me where I lay on the floor.

Solid. Real.

The shower attachment that would be fitted around the bath-tub in the years to come had not appeared yet. I filled the tub, lowered myself into the steaming water, soaked in it, grateful for the luxury.

I watched the steam drift up and out the window.

Watched it disappear.

I wandered down to the Woolworth's on Winchester. Candy, postcards, toys, bars of soap, chewing gum. Gold-filled rings that a baby could wear sold for a dime.

At the food counter I saw Jack sitting, talking to Teresa. I was several aisles away, unnoticed.

I watched him touch her hand. I watched her let him leave his hand there. I watched her smile, saw the way she looked at him.

I left before they saw me.

I had seen what I had suspected that first time I had seen them together. I had seen another of Jack Radey's secrets.

In the late afternoon, I was sitting on the veranda steps of the hotel when Jack came strolling down the street. He smiled and sat down beside me.

We sat in silence for a few minutes, letting our Canadian skin feel the Kentucky sunshine coming through the October clouds.

"You really go to work at the hospital?" I asked finally.

He nodded. "I go there. Do my job." He pulled a package of Lucky Strike cigarettes from his pocket, shook one loose, put it between his lips, lit it. "You don't smoke, right, Leo?"

"Right."

"Smart. Fifteen cents a pack. I must be nuts. I smoked Player's or Gold Crest back home. When you went to the States, everybody wanted you to bring back a pack of Luckies." He blew the smoke out in a stream into the sunlight. "The hospital," he said. "When the job's done, I leave. Do it as quickly as I can. Come back here. Then I do my real work." He leaned forward, placed his elbows on his knees. Then he looked at me. "What do you know about Toledo?"

I looked back at him. "I know what happened."

He waited.

"Drove through myself," I heard myself saying. "Heard the stories. Stan said you were there."

He inhaled on his cigarette.

"Fellow was either on one side or the other," I said.

"The right side or the wrong side," he finished.

I did the waiting this time.

"I was on the wrong side." The smoke drifted from his nostrils. "Took a man's job 'cause I wanted a job of my own. I didn't understand. Went into work one morning and this guy comes up to me and stands in my way. Little guy. Smaller than me. Thought there was going to be a fight. Thought maybe he was goin' to hit me. Guy says to me, 'You're either one stupid son of a bitch, or you're one mean fucker to do what you're doin'.' I had to decide which I was. I like to think I was just stupid." A silence. Then: "Biggest mistake of my life. Learned everything I needed to know from the experience."

"Nothing like making a mistake to make you smart."

He smiled. "I must be the smartest man on earth, then."

"Tell me about Marg," he said. "How's she doing?"

It's 1934, I thought. She'd be twenty-five years old. My sister Anne would be four. Ron was two. "Doing well," I said. "Kids keep her busy." I thought for a moment. "She's good at what she does. Being a mother. Loving her family."

He nodded. "She's like a little girl in a lot of ways, too."

I couldn't answer that.

"Naive." A pause. "But nice naive. Even though the worst shit happened to her—to all of us—she always thought everyone was really decent underneath. Had trouble believing bad things about people." He inhaled on his cigarette, exhaled. "Don't know how you get like that." Another pause. "Told me once when she was pregnant with Anne that she didn't understand how the baby was going to get out of her. She asked the doctor. It wasn't clear in her head." He looked at me. "Can you imagine?"

I was speechless. Another revelation. Something I could never know about my own mother unless she told someone, and I was somehow privy to it. Another of the secrets w   all carry around within us, unknowable to others. Unknowable to our own children.

"She once found a twenty-dollar bill on the floor of the local dairy when we were teenagers. Wouldn't keep it. Said it was probably some person's entire weekly pay. Turned it in to the girl behind the counter. Said the person would probably come back looking for it. I couldn't convince her that the girl was just gonna pocket it—that she'd just given away twenty dollars." He shook his head. "Good old Marg."

It rang true.

"I'm not like that," he said. He held the butt of the cigarette tightly between his thumb and index finger, inhaling sharply.

I thought of his easy acceptance of me, his trust in taking me to his room, his support of me in front of the others, just like his sister.

"Not like that at all," he said.

Jack looked at the sky. He looked to the east. The sun was clouded over. "Rain," he said. "It's comin'."

"Marg got married fast," he said.

"Sometimes things happen fast."

He thought about it. Then: "How's Tommy?"

"Works hard. Works for the *Globe* during the day. Gets up when it's still dark. He's in charge of all the boxes all the way up Yonge Street, past the city limits." I had heard the stories many times. "Evenings, he plays jobs with his guitar, banjo. Romanelli's Orchestra. The Royal York. Palais Royale on the Lakeshore. Plays on the boats that go across the lake and back. Money's good. Dead tired, though, from what I hear."

"Marg must be alone a lot." He looked at me strangely, inquisitive.

I thought of Jack with Teresa.

"It's not like that," I said.

He smiled, a bit embarrassed, but relieved.

"She's just a special person who's nice to everybody. Like you said."

He looked down.

"Your father," I said suddenly. "You should write to him."

Jack looked at me with surprise. Then he said, "We had a falling out. Don't get along too well." He paused. "Marg tell you about that?"

"Didn't exactly tell me. Just bits I picked up, listening."

"Like we were talking about. Marg can't see him for what he is. Only sees what she wants to see."

"Maybe she sees him perfectly."

He looked at me.

"You, too."

He was quiet.

"He's your father." I shrugged. "We don't get to pick our family. Our family happens to us."

He said nothing for a long time before he spoke. "I'll think about it," he said finally.

"You should keep writing to Marg. She loves your letters. Saves 'em."

He frowned.

"Keep writing."

"I will," he said. The frown deepened. "I definitely will."

At five that day, along with dozens of others, we had white beans boiled in water, two slices of bread, and a cup of tea.

12

Friday, October 12, 1934

AT 1:00 A.M. JACK CAME INTO THE ROOM. I SAT UP ON HIS BED, where I had been sleeping while he was at the hospital.

When he flicked on the light, I saw it on him at the same time I heard it through the open window.

His hair was plastered wetly to his head and the drips had formed at his chin. The shoulders of his shirt were soaked through.

We both listened to the steady drizzle on the pavement outside.

It was a steady downpour.

Jack looked out the window. "Need to talk to Stan," he said. "He knows the feel of this better than I do."

I was putting on my shoes.

Jack went through the door. I followed, closing it after me.

They were in the basement, gathered about the drain hole there: Stanley, Emmett, Henry, George, Jimmy.

Stan looked up when he heard us coming.

They stepped aside as Jack and I glanced down into the hole.

It had risen about six inches.

When I looked up, George met my eyes. "The Ohio," he said. "Lyin', waitin'."

We listened to the steady trickle of water into the pit, heavier now than I had heard it before.

"What do we do?" asked Jack.

Stanley looked at him, shrugged. "Keep diggin'."

"Pray," said Jimmy. He ran a dirty hand through his matted red hair.

The springs in the tunnel ran in rivulets around our ankles as we dug. Emmett spent most of the night checking and propping the vertical beams, shoring them up where water had eroded the firmness of their footings. He fixed additional horizontals beneath the tram tracks where the earth had begun to disappear.

The wetness turned most of the earth into mud, and each shovelful took on three times the weight.

By dawn we were exhausted.

The water in the pit had risen another four inches.

At noon, we sat on the veranda of the hotel and listened to the train pull into Ashland. Within an hour, we were able to watch as the armored car pulled up to the bank and began to unload the money.

The rain poured down steadily as the gray figures moved from truck to bank and back again.

When Jack went to his hospital job that evening, I went into the basement where Stan and George had already begun to work.

A small steady stream sluiced noisily down through the tunnel mud into the drain pit.

Even from where I stood at the base of the stairs, I could see that the hole was full.

13

Saturday, October 13, 1934

JACK CAME INTO THE TUNNEL SOMETIME BETWEEN 1:00 AND 2:00 A.M.

We were ankle-deep in water.

As the rain loosened the earth, the far end of the tunnel began to fall away in ever larger chunks under our assault—a phenomenon both exhilarating and frightening. We filled the tram what seemed like a hundred times, sending it back to the basement to be dumped.

The tracks were completely underwater.

As we burrowed deeper under the streets of Ashland, Emmett and Henry cut and built the supports from pine beams, shimmed and jockeyed them into place, fixing them with miners' care, knowing what was at stake.

Still, as the water swirled about the bases of the beams, even though nothing was said, the worry in their eyes was clear to all.

I thought of my solitaire games of years ago, the random flow of cards like the river beneath us.

* * * *

And another memory card turned over.

I had taken my nephew, Bill, to a Jays game. He was ten? Eleven? The tickets, from a scalper, had cost me a bundle. The parking, the hot dogs, the ice cream, the program.

The Jays beat the Angels.

On the street, on the way out, more sidewalk vendors hawked their wares.

Can I have a pennant? he asked.

I looked at them briefly, checked their price. The cheapest was $5.

No, I said, feeling cleaned out. Too expensive. We've spent enough already.

He took it with resolve.

Next time, I said.

He said nothing.

We went home.

And now, my back sore, sweat pouring down my brow, covered from head to toe in mud, beneath the streets of Ashland, Kentucky, somewhere in a past I do not understand, I wonder what I was thinking. There was no next time. I wonder what good that $5 is to me now.

I'd give anything, I think suddenly, looking into the glare from the bare light bulb, the sweat running into my eyes, to buy the pennant for him now.

And then the light bulb went out.

I blinked, its afterimage still burning into my eyes in the dark.

"Jesus Christ."

"What happened?"

"Quiet." A flashlight snapped on.

I squinted at the new glow. It was in Stanley's hand, attached by a chain to his belt.

The beam moved steadily about our surroundings, focusing finally on the electric wire that ran our lights. There was water dripping from the tunnel ceiling now, and the wire was covered in droplets.

Stanley started back along the tunnel.

We followed.

We lifted our feet carefully so as not to trip on the submerged tracks. The water swirled now at midcalf, rising.

About forty feet back along the tunnel, we saw what had happened. A small portion of the tunnel roof had collapsed, pulling down with it the electric cord. The wire angled down from in front of us to where it was buried beneath a pile of wet earth some two feet high. The earth covered the floor of the tunnel for about six feet.

We looked at it, looked at one another.

Stanley bent forward, pulled the end of the wire. "Hold this." He turned, detached the flashlight, and gave it to Jack. Then he crawled up on his knees atop the collapsed earth and pulled the wire loose for the six feet it was buried.

He stood on the opposite side of the pile, the cord in his hands. "Must've pulled a connection loose farther back."

"Ain't good," George said.

"Looks like we got some repairs to do," Stanley said.

We stared at him, standing in the glow of the beam from Jack's hand, the water building up closer to our knees.

It only took minutes to clear the floor of most of the fallen earth, to shovel it to the sides enough to uncover the submerged tracks. It reminded me of being a kid after a rainstorm, of damming up the flow of water rushing along the curb gutter, then breaking it open to let the buildup break free and disappear down the sewer.

But instead of disappearing, the water merely dropped a few inches, back to the level of midcalf.

We stared at the space in the ceiling above us where the earth had collapsed. I thought of the entire town sitting above us, of our frailty in the earth below.

I asked it, what was not being said: "Is this safe?"

For a moment there was only the sound of the droplets falling and the quiet rush of water about our legs.

"Mine's a mine," Stan said. "Tunnel's a tunnel. Ain't natural. Men ain't really supposed to be down here, doin' this. Always a risk."

"But the rain," I said.

"Make's it trickier," said George. "Like Stan says, though, it's the nature of the beast."

"I took two men out of a mine near the Panther Creek in West Virginia back in thirty-one," said Emmett. "Wasn't no rain. Just happened. Sometimes it just happens. Didn't mind workin' in the mines till then."

"I can take you to see this mausoleum in a cemetery outside Coal Mountain." Henry had been silent for hours until now. "Fella buried there spent his whole life underground. Said when he died he wanted to be buried above ground. Kinda to balance things out." He looked around. "Lots spend a lifetime below. Nothin' happens to 'em."

"But the rain," I said. "The water."

Their faces set grimly, in silence.

"Ought to work in shifts from now on," said George.

Stan nodded.

"No more'n three at a time in the tunnel," he continued. "Make sure there's always more on the outside than on the inside, in case another chunk collapses. Could dig us out, or get help. Be a safety measure."

"Makes sense," said Jimmy.

"It'll slow us up," said Emmett.

"Diggin's goin' well," said Stan. "Like Jimmy says, makes sense."

Emmett looked unconvinced.

"Till the rain stops," said Stanley.

Emmett hesitated, then nodded. "Makes sense, I guess," he agreed, finally.

I dug for a while longer with Jack and Stanley. The others took a break, becoming the safety crew.

"Know anything much about coal, Leo?" asked Stan, suddenly, after watching the others leave.

Sometimes we needed to talk just to hear the sound of human voices. Sometimes we just wanted the silence. This was one of those times for the voices.

I remembered it was 1934, searched for a memory that would fit. I remembered playing in the coal bin in the basement when I was a kid, remembered getting hell because I was coal black afterward. "Got a big old octopus furnace that opens its mouth and eats it up," I said. "Lot colder there. Burn it all winter." I remembered watching my father shovel it into the flames.

I heaved a shovelful of dirt into the tram, thought. "I watch the men pour coal down the chutes into the apartment buildings around the corner from where I live. Looking at them, their hands, their faces, I wonder how they ever get clean. Even handlin' it after it's been dug up seems like a hell of a job." I dug the shovel back into the wall, heaved again. "I remember a story my father told me. Told me about how his own father had a horse used to be out back of the house on Berkeley Street. Horse was used to pull the coal wagon my grandfather drove to deliver it in the area." I smiled wryly. "Don't know the same things about coal up in Canada as you do down here. We delivered it and burned it up, after you got it out of the ground.

Comes in by train. Sits in big cement silos." I rubbed my nose, smudging dirt across it. "Heard of black lung, but never saw it," I added.

Stanley wiped his brow, listening, watching me. "Hard to picture it gettin' all the way up there to Canada."

"My father says that old horse was a swayback. Says he had grass growing out of his back."

Stanley smiled.

"Ever hear of Father Coughlin?" asked Jack, topping off the tram, smoothing out the dirt with his shovel.

I straightened. "Matter of fact, I have."

"Ever actually hear him?"

I shook my head. "No," I said.

"Every Sunday. From Royal Oak, Michigan. Was in charge of buildin' the shrine there, to Saint Therese, the Little Flower. Till he started makin' people aware of things we should know, things that need sayin'."

I watched his face, in the shadows, become enlivened.

"Puts the international bankers right up there with the devil and the Communists."

Stanley had stopped and was listening now.

"The Union for Social Justice," said Jack. "He read us some statistics couple weeks ago that said the profits of the wealthy had increased sixty-six percent the last few years, while wages and salaries had dropped sixty percent in the same time."

"The Radio Priest," said Stanley, "gets eighty thousand letters a week. Poll taken at the radio station asked if folks wanted to hear his program. Hundred thirty-seven thousand said yes. Four hundred said no."

"Program's on Sundays," said Jack. "Goin' to miss it this Sunday, I expect. Might miss mass, too." He grinned at Stanley.

Stanley smiled back.

This Sunday. It was what we were here for.

*　*　*　*

That evening, after dinner, we sat in the parlor in front of the radio, sipping tea: myself, Jack, Stanley, Teresa, George, and Jimmy. The teapot sat on a crocheted doily on top of a mahogany coffee table. Beside the teapot lay a well-thumbed copy of the February 1934 issue of *Vanity Fair,* which looked all of its nine or ten months old. The cover featured a caricature of FDR as a Rough Rider, complete with chaps, hat, boots, scarf. He was riding a saddled outline of the U.S.A., his reins pulling on the snout up in Maine, his heels digging in down in the southwest. Easily taming the wild steed beneath him, he tipped his hat in the air and smiled.

It cost 35¢.

I touched it.

"Ever hear his Fireside Chats?" asked Stanley.

I looked up. He was watching me. I knew that he watched me a lot. "No," I said, sitting back, letting my fingers slip from its slick surface. I shrugged. "Canada, remember?"

"Course. I forgot. Don't think of it. Well," he continued, "it's his favorite way of sellin' his programs. Radio talks. Tries to make 'em sound informal. Likes to wait till folks are relaxing after dinner, till your food is digestin' nicely, so your brain isn't functionin' full tilt."

George chuckled. "Shoulda heard his first one. 'Bout a year ago. Told us all 'bout how the banks were bein' reorganized, how it was safer to put your money in 'em than to leave it under your mattress. Told us there would be no losses that possibly could have been avoided." He frowned, scratched his head. "Still puzzlin' that one over."

"Don't want other folks' money," said Stanley. He looked down at the magazine cover. Then he said, very softly: "Just Barbara's."

I sipped my tea. "Where are we in the tunnel?"

Stanley looked up. "Right underneath it," he said. "Right under the vault. We'll be through tomorrow."

"Drills and torches are ready to go," said Jimmy, speaking for the first time.

"What happens when they open the bank on Monday morning and find the money gone—see the hole, the tunnel?" I'm not sure I really believed we'd get there until I asked the question. I realized that I'd just been going along with them.

Stanley looked at Jack, then at George. They smiled. Then he said: "We think we got it figured out."

Jack leaned forward. The blue eyes, the white smile. He came alive. "Got a series of plans, Leo. None of them lead back here."

Teresa listened, quiet, wide-eyed, admiring.

Stanley was nodding, thinking. Then he looked from Jack to Teresa, watching.

I saw the look on Stanley Matusik's face as he watched the two of them, and realized that he knew.

I couldn't take my eyes from his face. I studied it, trying to read the thoughts behind it, trying to follow the river of his emotions.

As I watched him, his face became a puzzle, his eyes colorless. I watched for anger, resentment, jealousy. Instead I saw traces of sadness in the slackened muscles, a deep weariness in his carriage.

Jack looked at him.

"No. You go ahead," said Stan. He seemed suddenly to struggle with the tiredness, to shake it away, collect himself. "You tell it."

Jack smiled, excited, oblivious. "Emmett and Henry aren't here, you notice. They're part of another crew. They've been digging a shorter, smaller tunnel that's all set to join up at a right angle with ours just beneath the vault. Only got about three feet more to go. Been just sittin' there waitin' for us. Comes in from a sewer main beneath Winchester. We got it filled with clothes and stuff left behind by transients for the past six months. False trail, so they won't be looking for locals. They can inspect and scour it for weeks. Hundreds of false clues everywhere. Address books. Empty wallets with old IDs. Road maps, with places circled. Train schedules. You name it." His eyes shone.

"We got the last twenty feet of our own tunnel rigged to collapse where it meets the Winchester one," he continued. "Pull a couple of ropes, it disappears. They open up Monday morning, see everything cleaned out, see the hole, follow it down to the tunnel that leads into the main sewer, see all the stuff we put there, and that should be it. No reason at all for them to come looking for us. No reason even for any of us to have to leave the hotel, or Ashland."

"But won't they see the collapsed opening?" The questions spilled out of me. "Won't they be able to tell that there was a tunnel there? Won't they wonder where the covered tunnel went?"

"Emmett and Henry will fix that. They can smooth it over between now and Monday morning so's you'd never know there was one there," said George. "And if anyone suspected and decided to start digging it out, why they'd never be able to tell if it was a tunnel or not. And we can fill in and collapse the rest slowly over the next few days. Nothin'll lead back here. Ain't no one goin' to dig our tunnel back out after we bring her down. Too much work. Wouldn't make no sense. 'Specially with all them clues sitting in the other direction."

I didn't have much to say. They seemed to have covered all the bases.

Then we heard the thunder. It rumbled down from the east, rattled the windows.

The rain continued to bounce off the pavement outside.

All the bases except one, I thought.

* * * *

It was Saturday night. Most people went to the movies.

We'd all seen *King Kong*. We sat in the parlor, cradling teacups, and listened to "Your Hit Parade."

I watched Stanley.

He watched Teresa and Jack.

I began to feel light-headed. The parlor of the Scott Hotel came into focus as though through a wide-angle lens, curving at the edges.

Is any of this real, I wondered?

Will I ever see my father, my home, my job, Jeanne, or Adam again?

Where am I? What's happening?

I didn't know.

Below us, the Ohio River strove upward, trying to join the sky and the rain, squeezing us blindly in between.

14

Sunday, October 14, 1934

"Jack, George, and Jimmy are the first shift," said Stanley. "They should clear the earth right up to beneath the vault. Scrape it clean, so's we can see what we're doin'."

For the first time in front of me, Stanley unfolded onto the coffee table, atop the *Vanity Fair,* a working diagram of the tunnel, the secondary tunnel, the sewer system, all superimposed on a scale drawing of streets and buildings.

"Leo and I'll work the basement, pull the tram out by rope if we can, spread the dirt around best we can."

"Water's pretty high," said George. "Don't know if you'll be able to move the tram that way."

"We'll try it anyway. If we can't, we'll do whatever we have to. Whatever it takes."

In the basement, the water was deeper than we had dreamed. It swirled above the knees, restless, with no place to go.

"This'll never work," said George. "Too much water."

"Has to work," said Jack. He went first into the tunnel. Jimmy followed right behind him, taking his end of the long

181

rope, letting it uncoil like a water snake behind him as he disappeared.

George looked at us, then focused on Stan. "Too much water," he said again. Then he said what he was thinking: "We should wait a month."

Stanley's eyes did not see him. They seemed to be following the sound of the men wading down the tunnel. "We're right there," he said. "Right under it. It's ours."

George looked at me, then back at Stanley.

"Rain might even help." Stanley Matusik's eyes glazed. "Make it easier to collapse the tunnel afterward. No sign of any kind. Bury it forever."

George heard the same illogic in the voice that I heard and looked to me suddenly for support.

"Maybe George is right," I said.

Stanley did not even look at me. "Too late," he said. "Everything's too late. What's gonna happen is gonna happen."

He stared down the tunnel.

George turned and went after Jack and Jimmy.

We were able to retrieve the tram with its first load of earth. But when we had emptied it, before we could tug the rope on its other end in signal to haul it away, it was clear our system wouldn't work anymore.

The water continued to rise and, empty of weight, the tram car became unstable—not light enough to float, not heavy enough to ride the tracks.

"They try pullin' it back, it'll tip on its side. Fill up with water," said Stanley.

"I think you're right."

"Better tell them." He started to wade toward the tunnel.

"I'll come with you," I said.

"Don't have to. You can wait here."

"I'm coming." I slogged after him into the tunnel.

* * * *

Sometimes we remember everything with unusual clarity. Other times, it seems blurred, and we wish we were privy to some kind of instant replay, some way of studying an event to see how it happened, what happened, to try to understand it.

I don't know exactly what happened. I try to replay it in my head, but I can't see it clearly. In my mind I feel the water around my legs, feel the mud of the walls with my hand as I walk along, squint into the glare of bulbs.

Then suddenly it is dark. There is the feel of stale air on my face, blown as with a bellows, then I hear the muffled splash far up the tunnel at the same time I feel the walls shudder under my hand. The water stirs with new bubbles. A wave washes up toward my waist as it surges past me, ricocheting its way into the basement where it will crash around crazily without escape.

In the dark I stand there, knowing Stanley is somewhere beside me. Knowing that everything has gone bad.

The flashlight beam snapped on in Stanley's hand, darting crazily about the walls as he ran ahead of me through the water.

I ran after him, tripped, fell, got up, ran again.

The beam of light stopped at the wall of mud in front of us. Jack, George, and Jimmy were in there somewhere—under it or behind it.

I saw Jack's eyes, my mother's eyes, erupt like startling blue flares in my brain, arcing from the past to the present, and back to the past.

Stanley, Emmett, Henry, and I dug for the next fourteen hours straight. We burrowed a narrow path ten feet into the fallen mud without sensing any end to it.

When the water was above our waists, a section of tunnel some dozen feet or so behind us collapsed, leaving only a foot or so of air space above it. We shone our lights back along its top surface. The collapsed portion was only a six-foot span— a segment between supports.

The trapped water around us was rising rapidly.

We turned our efforts on the earth behind us, digging with energy we didn't know we had left, scraping a path along the top of the collapsed mud that would allow us to crawl over it.

With the water at our chests, we heaved ourselves up and inched our way out of our own plight, sliding down into the water and mud on the other side.

In the basement, exhausted, we tried to collect our thoughts.

"Have to go back," said Emmett.

We looked to Stanley. His face showed nothing. "Can't," he said. "Not now. Too much water." A pause. "We need rest, food, too."

"We can't leave them there," I said.

Stanley looked at me.

"What about the other tunnel?" I asked. I looked to Emmett and Henry.

Henry shook his head. "Runs off the sewer," he said. "Sewer's full. Everything's flooded. You'd need diving equipment. Even then, full of water like this, whole goddamn thing could come down on you in an eye blink." He looked down the tunnel in front of us. "This one, too."

"What do we do, then?" I asked. I heard my voice rise a notch.

No one answered.

The water, thick with its mud and power, flowed relentlessly out of the darkness around us.

By Sunday night, the water filled the basement completely.

15

Monday, October 15, 1934

THE WATER CREPT UP OVER THE CURBS ONTO SIDEWALKS. BY DAWN, the town was beginning sandbagging operations.

The bank did not open for general business that day. But it did open special at 10:00 A.M. for the armored car that pulled up in front of it.

I watched from the veranda as the rain poured down steadily and the gray figures moved from bank to truck and back again, gathering the money, escorting it to the train and out of Ashland before it, too, sank beneath the water.

It rained all day. The streets disappeared.

That evening, I stood knee-deep in water on Winchester Avenue, hands in my pockets, the rain running off my chin, down my neck, into my eyes, feeling where the pavement had buckled slightly beneath my feet, facing the Second National Bank.

Jack, I thought.

Jack.

And then it was over.

Everything changed.

16

They remain shadows . . . shadows whose few remaining words and acts I have invented. Perhaps I only wanted their forgiveness for having forgotten them.

I remember their deaths, but not their lives. Yet they're inside me, flowing unknown in my blood and moving unrecognized in my skull.

—MARGARET LAURENCE
The Diviners

1

THE AIR CHANGED.

The water was gone. The rain had stopped.

The wind blew warm and sultry.

I looked about me, at the present, at the hot August night of 1984.

I was back.

The lightning flashed in sheets in the sky, and I stood, as I had that night, outside the First National Bank and Trust building, looking into the smiling face and warmth that was Jack Radey.

"It's hot here," I heard him say. "But I like it. I like the possibilities." He stared at me, silhouetted in the radiance from a streetlight, a young man, confronted with his future. "A man can make something of himself down here. Anything can happen." He moved closer so that I could see the glow of hope on his face. "Do you know where Ashland is? Do you know where I could go from here?"

I didn't know what the answer was. I didn't know anything.

"God . . . " He ran his hand through black curly hair. "Anywhere," he said. There was a flicker of lightning, like a strobe.
"Anywhere." Then he turned and stared at the mountains, at
the east. "It's like the jumping off point to anywhere." He
paused. "I'm on the edge of the Virginias, the Carolinas. I could
go right through to Richmond or Norfolk, or up to Washington, Baltimore, Atlantic City. It's all ahead of me." He turned
to face me again. "You tell Margaret I'm fine."

I nodded slightly, feeling his presence everywhere.

"Tell her everything's fine. Tell her I miss her." He offered
his hand. I took it. His eyes sparkled.

"Tell Father I'm fine, too."

I nodded again. "I will."

He smiled openly, warmly. "Nice meeting you, Leo."

I smiled in return. "Margaret wants you to stay in touch."

"I will," he said.

And then he was gone.

It happened like that.

The moment of purity and insight and belief and hope and
regret and possibility folded up and vanished into the stillness.

I looked down at the cracks in the sidewalk, the shallow depression at my feet.

I went back to room 8 at the Scott Hotel. For most of the night
I sat in the blue upholstered easy chair, staring out the window
into the darkness, seeing nothing, seeing everything.

I think I fell asleep. I'm not sure.

I'm not sure of much anymore.

In the night, as before, perhaps as always, what seemed to
be dreams may have been real, what seemed real may have
been a dream.

In the morning I went to the basement of the Scott Hotel

and stood on a cement floor. Where the drain pit had been was a proper metal grill fixed in the floor. Everything was dry, reasonably modern.

I stared at poured concrete walls. The entrance to the tunnel was gone.

"Who are you?"

I turned to see Stanley Matusik, balding and timeworn, standing at the foot of the stairs behind me.

"I'm just who I said I was."

"I know you. From somewhere."

I nodded. "Maybe you do."

He looked at me. The eyes searched. "You know, don't you."

"I think so."

"How?"

"I just know."

He knew it was true. "Been over fifty years." Then he asked. "What do you know?"

"I know it didn't work. I know they're in there. Jack, Jimmy, George." I glanced at the wall where the tunnel had been.

"Yes and no," he said.

My senses sharpened. Maybe I didn't know.

"You know about the rain. About the flood." Statements, not questions.

"Yes."

"Whole goddamn thing came down. Water turned everything to mud, everywhere. Filled both tunnels solid, like they was never there. When it stopped, when it finally receded, when everything dried up, you couldn't even tell there'd been anything but solid ground there ever." He walked over to the concrete wall, stared at the opening in his mind. "We dug the whole thing out again. Me, Henry, Emmett, and some others. Took us eight weeks to do it properly. By then, rumors was goin' 'round. Folks in town seemed to know what had hap-

pened. Jimmy and George's families must've talked. We asked
'em not to." He shrugged. "What can you do? Don't really
blame 'em."

He turned and looked at me.

I waited.

"We found Jimmy and George. Found their bodies."

His stare became a probe as he studied my face.

"Never did find Jack."

I realized that I had stopped breathing.

"He wasn't there."

"What do you mean he wasn't there?"

"Gone. Don't know what happened to him."

"That's impossible."

"Yes," he said. "I know."

He walked with me up the stairs and out into the morning air.
We sat on the veranda.

A steady drizzle had started. Steam rose off the sidewalk.

"Could tell it was goin' to rain, the last coupla nights." He
folded his hands in his lap, looked at me, looked at the sky.

"Maybe you just missed him. Maybe he got washed away."
I tried what I had been thinking aloud, tried them to make sure.

He shook his head.

"I don't understand."

"Not sure I do either. Man goes into the earth, doesn't come
out." Again, he shook his head. "We made certain, before we
sealed it all up. Took Jimmy and George to their families. They
buried them in family plots on their properties out of town.
Like I said, rumors were flyin'. Nobody asked too many questions, though. There was enough talk that we forgot the whole
idea of the bank, the money. Wouldn't've worked no more."
He stared hard at my face. "Like there's somethin' missin' when
I look at you, Leo. Like there's somethin' I can't remember. Like
you're a piece of the puzzle, but I can't fit it in."

Whatever had happened to me, I realized, hadn't happened to him the same way.

He studied, probed, frowned. "Can't get hold of it. Like a wisp in my head, then it's gone. Like I should know somethin' more about you. But it's fuzzy. It's blurry." He was quiet for several seconds. Then: "It couldn't've been, though, could it?"

"No," I said. "It couldn't."

"Mind plays tricks on you. 'Specially when you get old."

"Plays tricks on everyone," I said.

"Dug a new basement out in forty-seven," he said. "After the war. Put jacks under the whole building. Poured a new concrete foundation." He pondered. "Our scheme, everything we did before that, seems like madness when I think about it now."

"Was the times," I said. "There was a kind of madness everywhere." I thought of George walking twenty-five miles looking for a job. I thought of Henry, whose little girl's hair fell out. Of Emmett, whose little boy died of scarlet fever.

"What happened to Henry? To Emmett?"

"Died," said Stanley. "Both of them died back in the sixties. Long time ago. Henry had cancer. Emmett just seemed to die. Heart, I think."

"So it's over."

"I'm alive. Ain't over in my head. Long's I'm alive," he said, "it ain't over." His eyes weakened. Thinking. Weighing.

I remembered the looks he had given Jack and Teresa, his knowledge of something between them. And I realized that I could never know what his motives had been for sending Jack into the tunnel that last time.

Or whether he knew himself.

2

MIDAFTERNOON, I STOOD, FACING THE CLIFFS ON THE OPPOSITE shore of the Ohio. Then I sauntered in the warm rain to the park behind the library at 17th and Central, to stare at the mounds of the three Indian graves. I sat on the park bench, thinking about entire villages beneath my feet, of their lives and loves and commerce thousands of years ago.

Of the layers beneath us all.

When the sky began to clear and the rain let up and I became more aware of my wet clothing, I realized that it was time to go.

Glancing one last time at the mounds, I left.

In my room I packed my things. My eyes lighted on the microwave, the bar fridge, and I thought of Emma's efforts to accommodate me, to encourage me to stay.

Emma.

And it hit me for the first time.

I stepped into the parlor and gazed in wonder at the child's portrait in the elongated oval frame.

Yes, I thought.

"It's me."

I turned to see Emma Matusik standing behind me.

"It was taken in nineteen forty-one. I was six years old."

I thought of how she had wanted me to stay, of how Jack had wanted me to stay. You could see him in her eyes. You could see the sudden, startling blue. You could see the cheekbones, the dark curly hair. Jack. My mother. The Radey features.

"Did you find Jack Radey?" she asked.

Hotels, rivers, tunnels spanning two countries flooded into

my head. I saw men digging, women working, and Jack and Teresa together, stealing what they could from life.

"Yes," I said, and felt my heart swell in my chest as I looked at her, at my cousin.

"I needed to find him, too," she said.

I nodded, understanding.

"My mother told me enough of the story when she was ready to tell it, when I was ready to hear it. I was in my twenties. I found an old book from the local library at the back of a shelf in my mother's closet. I was looking for one of her sweaters for her. I picked it up, wondered why it hadn't been returned. There was a photograph of a young man between its pages. It was a photo of Jack. He used to take pictures, you know."

I knew.

"Mother didn't keep any other mementos. It didn't seem right. She and my father built a good life together. They managed to live with it."

"Does Stanley know?"

"Mother says he doesn't. But I think he does. He's never said anything, though. He's a good man." She paused. "I love him very much."

"Does your mother still have the photo? The book?"

"She gave them to me. I have them."

I waited.

"Would you like to see them?"

"Yes," I said.

Carefully, I opened the fifty-year-old copy of Maugham's *The Moon and Sixpence,* held the yellowed black-and-white photograph in my fingers, and lingered over the incredible piercing eyes and the dazzling white smile for the last time.

17

Writing letters is actually an intercourse with ghosts,
and by no means just with the ghost of the addressee but
also with one's own ghost, which secretly evolves inside
the letter one is writing.

—FRANZ KAFKA
Letters to Milena

1

JEANNE APPROACHED ME ALONG THE CURVED COUNTER WITH HER pencil poised over a yellow receipt pad. Her smile had started the second she caught sight of me coming through the doors. "You still hungry, fella? Can't get enough of Kentucky cooking?" The strand of hair fell out from behind her ear.

"You just whetted my appetite."

"Glad to hear it."

"Interested in a little excitement?"

"Fast lane. Life on the edge. It's where I live. Look around you." She jerked her head to indicate the nearly empty store.

"How far's Cincinnati?"

" 'Bout ninety miles."

"If you can get out of here a little early, you, me, and Adam could be sitting down in some good seats at Riverfront Stadium by game time. The Cardinals are in town for a set. Should be a good game. You know much about baseball?"

"Hardly a damn thing."

"Want to go?"

She was undoing her apron. "I'd like to see them try to stop me."

It was a hot, humid night, perfect for baseball. The Reds won on a line single to right field in the ninth by Dave Parker. We ate hot dogs and ice cream, and bought the overpriced programs.

On the way out of the stadium, I paid $5 for a pennant for Adam and watched his face light up.

Jeanne put her arm through mine and pulled me to her tightly.

It was past midnight when we got back. Jeanne got Adam to bed, then went with me downstairs to sit on the steps of the veranda.

A summer night in Ashland was everything a summer night should be.

When I looked at Jeanne, she was watching me. "Something's happened."

"Yes," I said. "Something has happened."

"You found your uncle."

I tilted my head to one side, trying to decide what to say that would make sense. "Yes and no."

She waited.

"Found out he isn't here anymore. Found out he's probably dead."

She leaned her head against my shoulder.

"I found his daughter."

"Any other family?"

I thought about it. "Not that I know of," I said.

"She living here?"

"Yes."

"Married?"

"No."

"Her mother?"

"Never married my uncle. Married someone else. Still married to him." I paused. "It's complicated."

Her hand covered mine. We sat in silence for a while. Then Jeanne looked up at the night sky. "Rain's passed."

I looked up, too.

"You're leaving, aren't you." A statement.

I looked down, nodded.

She squeezed my hand. "We had a good time."

"I got a job back home. Family."

"I know."

"Have to go back."

"I know."

I didn't know what else to say.

"Will you stay with me tonight?" she asked.

"I'd like that," I said. "I'd like that very much."

2

I LEFT ASHLAND THE NEXT MORNING, CROSSED THE OHIO, WENT along 52 to 23, and north. I saw a small family cemetery high up on a hill and thought of how much more natural it was to bury one's dead like that than the way it is for most of us now.

I thought of George and Jimmy.

I had lunch at the Court Café in Bucyrus.

Later, because it was hot, and because I was tired, I pulled off Route 4—the Lincoln Highway—just south of 20, had a Pepsi at a gas station, and read a poster for the Seneca Caverns, the ones I had read about on my way to Ashland.

I got back in the car and followed the signs. Fifteen minutes later I pulled into a modest picnic area, parked, and walked into the rickety gift shop. The sign above the shop announced: Enter the Caves in Here.

I told myself I needed the break. I bought a ticket for the next tour.

There were about twenty of us.

A local high school girl led us down the poured cement stairs. I felt the temperature drop into the fifties, felt the sweat cool on my skin. I left the upper world behind.

The cavern was not a solution cavern. It had been formed by an earthquake, millions of years ago—a giant crack in the earth. The roofs and floors, it is pointed out, would fit perfectly into one another if compressed.

The high school girl delivered her well-rehearsed speech at each point of interest. When we reached the bottom we were introduced to "Old Mist'ry River," which, we were told, had defied all attempts to measure its depth or locate its source. The stream's only inhabitants were amphipods—half-inch-long shrimplike creatures.

I asked her if it ever rose up higher into the caverns.

"During freshet thaw," she said. "Ten years ago it rose right up to within ten feet of the entranceway. But," she added, "it always recedes again. It always drops back to its proper level."

I nodded, remembering my mother's words. *Jack was here. And my father.*

Turning, we retraced our steps, up out of the cavern. I wanted to go home.

At Detroit, I crossed the border into Windsor.

In Toronto, life went on.

I returned to my job, visited my father occasionally. He had been right, I guess. In the kitchen, that day before I left, he had simplified it. Things have to be settled, or they never go away.

* * * *

At first, I phoned Jeanne weekly. Then it was twice a week.

August became September. The nights became cooler, but I still tossed, slept restlessly, alone.

By late September, we were talking every night.

When the phone rang, I expected it to be Jeanne.

It was my father.

"Another letter came," he said.

I had thought it had ended. I had thought it was over. "From Ashland? From Jack?"

"From Jack. But not from Ashland. Come and see."

I saw the river rise up one more time, saw it carrying bodies, filling caverns.

I hung up and left.

The yellowed envelope had the two-cent Washington red and the green one-cent counterpart. It was postmarked Bucyrus, Ohio, December 23, 1934. It was stationery from the Highway again, the same place as one of the first batch of letters that had arrived before my trip south.

"On the Nation's Main Thoroughfare. The Lincoln Highway."

My father handed me the letter that had been inside. It was dated the same as the postmark on the envelope.

Dear Margaret:

Sorry I haven't written for so long, but I've been more than a little busy. And I've always been a little careless, as you well know.

Things didn't work out in Ashland. You have no idea how I wish they had. It's kind of complicated, and a long story—but there was some trouble (nothing that you should worry about) and I figured it was certainly time to go.

Bucyrus is pretty. I'm doing lots of manual labor, and have dis-

covered that shoveling manure here smells the same as it does every-where else. Odd jobs are scarce, but so far I can make enough for food, a place to stay, and a pack of cigarettes. What more could a fella want?

How I got here—now there's a story. But I'll save it for another time. Your little brother has managed to get out of a tight scrape and land on his feet. I guess I'm learning to survive. Father would be proud of me.

I trust Father is well.

You know, Marg, I'm beginning to miss Toronto. There's lots of times when I sit here in my room and think back to Berkeley Street. It wasn't so bad, you know? And remember Margueretta Street? And High Park? Honest to God, I don't think I know what I'm looking for anymore, Marg. I guess I just came back to this place out of habit, cause it was a place I'd been before. Last time I was here, I complained that the town was dead and that nothing happened. This time it seems just fine for now. Maybe I'm gettin' old, and can sit on the park benches with the old-timers better now.

Actually, it's the fact that Xmas is only two days away that's got to me. I miss everyone dearly, and feel kind of alone right now. I wish I could see you again, but it isn't in the cards right now. Remember how we used to string the popcorn with Mother, while Father would sit and smile and smoke his cigar? Gee, I must be gettin' sentimental. That was a long time ago.

I'm coming back to Toronto someday, Marg. You can bet on it. I want to see everyone. I still want to make something of myself, cause I know I can.

Think of me Xmas morning, when you and Tommy and the kids are opening your presents.

I'm sending along a little something for everyone for Xmas. Buy something nice for yourself and for the kids. And I'd like to ask a favor. Could you send the enclosed to Teresa Matusik, c/o The Scott Hotel, Ashland, Kentucky? I don't want to send it myself, cause too many questions might be asked. So if you can keep it for a while till you get to Port Dover next summer and mail it from there. That way, it wouldn't have a Toronto postmark on it, and that's important to me. The whole thing is kind of private, if you know what I mean.

Speaking of Ashland, I met a friend of yours there. His name's Leo. Nice fella. Say hello to him for me.

And say hello to Tommy and Ronny and Anne and everyone else. And say "hello" to Father. I find myself thinking a lot about him. I think maybe I've been too hard on him. I guess he's had things happen to him I'm just beginning to understand.

I'll try to keep in touch better, but you know how a fellow slips up.

Lots of Love,
Jack

My father handed me two faded postal money orders, for twenty American dollars each.

I looked at them. One was made out to my mother. The other was made out to Teresa Matusik.

Beauty and mystery, I thought, sensing pinpoints of light in the darkness. The twin stars in all our night skies.

3

I STAYED WITH MY FATHER THAT NIGHT. I SLEPT IN MY OLD ROOM, which neither he nor my mother had bothered to change much in twenty-odd years. The bookcase I had built was still there. The bunk beds in which my brother and I had slept had been disassembled, though, and one of them had undoubtedly drifted into the hands of someone in the family, along with the Hudson's Bay red-and-black trapper blanket that was an integral part of each unit. But the other one was still there, complete with its heavy woolen cover.

I lay beneath it, feeling its weight, its security, placed my hands behind my head and stared up into the darkness of a time gone by, waiting for the morning, waiting for whatever would happen next.

Squeezed out of the earth, I thought. The mud, the water, the tunnels. Jack was still out there. Somewhere. Moving across America.

It was true. I believed it.

The truth was beside me, on the night table: the money orders. The letter.

It was also inside me, moving in my own subterranean tunnels, flowing in the rivers, flooding me.

My father was good enough not to phone me at work until near the end of the day. Otherwise I'd never have been able to get anything done. But at four o'clock, the call came.

"Another one, Leo."

I didn't ask anything. "I'll be by on my way home."

It was from Toledo—the same address as before: 117–17th Street. It was dated April 30, 1935.

> Dear Margaret:
> This one's just a short note to keep in touch. I went out with a friend for a drink today because it was my birthday. You were the only one who ever remembered. Even Father used to forget. I'm 24 today, Marg. So how come I feel like I'm about 50 years older? I guess too many things have happened, and I seem to have lost so much.
> The friend I went out with was Mac. Remember I told you about him, and his new baby? Well, things are pretty tough for them now, as he is now out of work. I feel real sorry for them. Some days I just don't know what any of us are "gonna" do.
> Today's Tuesday. I went to Mass on Sunday. Been missing it too much. Next thing you know, I'll have to go to confession. Don't know

where I'll start my list of "sins." The priest better cancel whatever he has planned for the rest of the day, that's for sure.

I'm keeping busy. Not much work here though.

I miss everybody.

I think I'll be here awhile. Maybe you could send me Father's address. I think I might write him, when I get a chance.

> *Lots of Love,*
> *Jack*

It took a week for the next one to arrive. It was, as I was beginning to suspect it might be, from the Vermont Hotel, on West Columbia, in Detroit.

Jack was coming north. He was coming home.

It was dated August 21, 1935.

Dear Margaret:

Happy Birthday! I realize this won't get to you till after your birthday, but better late than never, right? Sorry to have been out of touch for so long. Gee, I always seem to be apologizing for not comin' up to snuff. I guess I'll never change.

I remember telling you how much I loved being here the last time I wrote, and how it would break my heart to have to go back to Toronto. How times change, eh? Even Hartican's gone out of business. Everybody seems to be in trouble, so I guess you could say I'm in good company.

I miss Toronto more and more. Don't be surprised if I show up on your doorstep sometime real soon, hat in hand. You wouldn't turn me away, would ya?

I feel real strange, Marg. I feel like I'm looking back on things, instead of seeing them straight on. I don't know how to describe it. I miss Ashland, too, you know. But I don't see how I can ever go back. By the way, I hope you sent that money order to Teresa, like I asked, maybe from Port Dover this summer. I miss her, too. But it wasn't "gonna" work. Sometimes I feel real bad about it all and how it ended. But that's another story.

I got something surprising to tell you. I got a letter from Father. I don't know how he found me, but he did. Said he'd like me to come home. He's a man of few words, and the letter must have been quite a strain to write. I was quite touched by it, and wrote him back. There are some bridges to mend there, but I'm "gonna" try. I know it's what you've always wanted for him and me, so I wanted to tell you. Think of it as my birthday present to you.

I still like to visit the Shrine here at Royal Oak. When I get to Toronto, I'll bring you a rose from the garden there.

Take care, Marg. And say "hello" to everybody.

Hope I see you soon.

> Lots of Love
> Your brother,
> Jack

I placed the letter on the kitchen table. My father was sitting at the other end.

"Things have to be settled," he said.

I looked at him. I felt shaky. I had to sit down. "Or they never go away," I finished, my voice a whisper.

Then I closed my eyes and saw my mother's hand open on the hospital bed, saw her fingers unfold, saw the fresh red rose from the shrine at Royal Oak fall out, and heard her voice, an echo, thinly, again, always. *Jack was here. And my father.*

Jack, I thought. Jack.

The river of images flowed through my brain.

I still did not open my eyes. I tried to think, tried to let what I was feeling crystallize into something hard and clear. Instead I saw ghosts, time warps, delusions, madness. Jack was as much here and now as he was there and then. As he had always been. As he would be tomorrow.

He had come home, however briefly, as he had said. As my mother had said.

I put my hand to my forehead. Finally, squeezing my eyes tighter, I saw, with perfect clarity, Jack and his father at Margaret's bedside, holding her hands, touching her face, smiling, seeing past the body that was dying, staring into the enduring heart of what she had once been and dreamed of being—of what we have all once been and dreamed of being, at that moment, that single moment, when our rose is in its full, vibrant bloom.

18

Memory is a transcendental function. Its objects may be physical bodies, faces ... but these are shot with luminosity ... So though we can't perceive 'soul' or 'spirit' firsthand it seems to me that this is precisely the phenomenon we summon back by way of an exercise of memory. And why the exercise of memory at certain times in our lives is almost too powerful to be borne.

—JOYCE CAROL OATES
Facts, Visions, Mysteries: My Father, Frederic Oates

1

CANADIAN THANKSGIVING, I EXPLAINED TO JEANNE OVER THE
phone, was celebrated earlier than the American one. In 1984,
it fell on Monday, October 8.

There was no direct air passage from Toronto to Ashland.
I booked a flight after work on USAir from Toronto to Huntington, West Virginia, Friday, October 5.

When I landed, I made two phone calls. One was to the
Scott Hotel, the other was to Jeanne. I asked her if we could
keep Saturday clear for the whole day, for something special.
What? she asked. Adam is included, I said. We'll take a little
trip.

The phone line crackled with anticipation at both ends.

Then I drove my rented car the fifteen miles or so along the
Ohio to Ashland.

It was still light when I pulled up in front of the Scott
Hotel.

Emma sat beside me on the wine-colored sofa with the needlepoint pillows at each end.

"I've got some things I think you should have." I handed her Jack's letters, all of them. Detroit, Toledo, Bucyrus. Ashland. And back again.

She held them in her hands, stared at them, set them down in her lap.

"One of them's got something in it for your mother." I pictured the money order. "But I think you should have it."

Her eyes became the eyes that I had seen in Jack's face when he had admitted to me the truth about his letters to his sister that day on the porch swing.

"I think we should leave Teresa and Stanley alone. Not stir up the ghost between them."

She looked at the letters in her lap, looked at me. "Thank you."

It seemed best. It seemed like what Jack would have wanted if he'd known he had a daughter.

"I have to go," I said.

Her hands tightened on the letters. "Will I see you again?"

"I think so. I've got friends here."

She smiled weakly.

"Family, too." I touched her arm. "The place gets into your blood."

And it was true. Family, I thought, looking at her clutching the letters. Woven together with threads of steel. Sometimes the threads bend and twist, and you have to hammer them back into shape. But they don't tear. They don't break.

Jack was in Toronto, with his father, somehow, somewhere. I had seen the rose, fresh and alive, in my mother's hand.

I stood on the sidewalk outside the Scott and gazed at the "luxury accommodations in the heart of the city" on the north side of Winchester. The Ashland Plaza Hotel had opened. Glancing back at the Scott, it was clear that its days were numbered.

I didn't know if there would be any more letters, from Ashland or anywhere else. I had no way of knowing what the future would bring.

It didn't matter.

I had no way of knowing what the past would bring either.

I felt good. Adventure wasn't in the past or the future. It was right here. Living my life. Now.

Jeanne and Adam were waiting for me on the veranda when I pulled up in front of the house. I shook hands with Adam, then put my arms around Jeanne and held her. She was wearing the perfume, the subtle Southern scent from the evening of the Chimney Corner Tea Room, and nothing that I could remember had ever smelled so good.

"Got a trip planned for tomorrow," I said. I took a swig of warm beer from the long-necked bottle of Bud and digested the look on Adam's face. We were back outside, sitting on the steps beneath a warm October sky.

"Where?" he asked.

"Got to get up early. Take us half the day to get there. We'll stay over in a motel tomorrow night, come home Sunday. My flight doesn't leave till Monday."

"Cincinnati? Baseball?"

"Nope. Not this time."

It was Jeanne's turn to become curious. She had thought she had guessed it, too. She balanced her beer bottle with a hand on her knee. "Where?" she asked.

"We'll have a picnic while we're there. We'll make sandwiches tonight."

Adam drank his Coke, eyes jumping from one to the other of us.

"I've been studying maps, brochures," I said. "Kentucky travel guides. Places to go, see. You know."

They waited. Jeanne smiled, watching Adam, her happiness evident.

"Ever been in a cave?" I asked Adam.

There was genuine surprise on his face. The expression on Jeanne's face wasn't far behind.

"No," he said.

I looked at Jeanne.

"Can't say that I have," she said with some wry amusement. Her eyes held mine warmly.

"Guess you could say they've become a bit of an interest of mine. Kentucky's shot through with some of the best anywhere. Got more than any other state. Over three thousand of them. Crystal Onyx Cave. Diamond Caverns. Just across the state line, West Virginia's got Lost World Caverns. You even got Carter Caves about thirty miles west of here."

"Is that where we're going?" Adam was smiling now, catching on.

"Nope," I said. "It's a surprise. Farther." I moved my hands apart the way someone does when describing a fish just caught. "Bigger."

"Man flies down from Canada, takes us on a mystery tour," said Jeanne.

"Wear walking shoes. Bring a coat." I looked at Jeanne, at Adam, smiled back at both of them, glad I was here.

2

WE LEFT AT DAWN AND TOOK 64 TO LEXINGTON, STOPPED AND ATE breakfast at a Bob Evans Restaurant in the city, then got onto the Blue Grass Parkway to Elizabethtown. From there we went south on 65.

"Where are we going?" asked Jeanne, finally. "Are you going to tell us?"

"Trust me," I said.

Adam giggled in the backseat.

Shortly before noon, we reached Mammoth Cave National Park, the longest cave systems ever discovered on earth.

"I've been reading about it," I told them as we pulled into the vast parking area. Buses from around the country were massed at various locations amid the sea of cars. "There's two hundred ninety-four miles, charted on five levels."

"Is it free?" asked Adam.

"Reasonable rates," I said. "I bought the tickets through a Ticketron outlet before I left Toronto."

"You're kiddin', " said Jeanne. Then she thought about it. "Like a Broadway play."

"Bigger than a Broadway play."

I stopped the car. "You got that lunch, partner?"

Adam banged his fist on the cooler on the seat beside him. Then he looked out at the picnic areas.

"I'm hungry."

"Me, too," he said.

I looked at Jeanne. She laughed.

"All cave tours are walking trips. There's seven to choose from. From half a mile to five miles, from one and a half hours to a half day."

"Jesus." Jeanne swallowed the bite of her ham-on-rye before continuing. "You're not going to make us walk five miles, are you?"

"No." I chuckled. "Sounds a bit much even for someone as incredibly fit as I am."

Adam giggled.

"Medium tour. Don't want the kid to strain himself."

He poked me in the ribs, still giggling.

* * * *

Cave temperature was always fifty-four degrees, we were told. Most in the group of more than a hundred put on coats. Then we strolled through the entranceway, disappeared beneath the earth.

We went through huge rooms, winding passageways, saw towering formations, delicate onyx flowers, waterfalls, streams, pools. We went down ramps, up stairways, entered soaring caverns, inspected milky stalactites, stalagmites, flowstone, limestone pendants, sparkling geological snowdrifts, rainbow coral.

Ever downward.

At the bottom, we entered the Mammoth Cave, the biggest, the best known.

It took my breath away.

Peering upward, I could not see its roof.

Darkness in every direction, in spite of the lighting system.

It was an opening in the earth that staggered the imagination, a space left behind millions of years ago by some dark, vanished sea, dwarfing us all.

I felt humbled, lost. I tried to imagine the first ancient discoverers of the cave, the fear, the awe.

The voice of the tour guide brought me back. "I'm going to turn the lights off," she said, "for just one minute. Don't move and don't speak. We want you to experience absolute darkness, just to see what it's like. You won't be able to see your hand in front of your face."

There was some nervous laughter.

"Ready?"

Jeanne stood on my left, Adam on my right. I placed my hand on her shoulder, left my right hand dangling.

The lights went out, and we stood there in total darkness. The seconds stretched out. Time stopped.

I could hear my heart hammering loudly in my blood. I thought of my mother. I thought of Jack, sitting in hotel rooms across America, softening his perception of his father. I thought of my grandmother, of her last years, of my brothers and sisters, of my own father, his hair impossibly white, sitting at the green arborite kitchen table with his hand in his belt, of the ancient money order made out to my mother, that I would carry in my wallet from now on. I thought of Ashland, where dreams die and are born again.

In the darkness.

There were decisions to make. I had my life to live.

Toronto. Ashland. Toronto. Ashland.

Jeanne. Jeanne.

Adam. Adam. Aidan.

Then, in the lightless space of that vanished sea below the earth, in the darkness, faced with the same terror and beauty, hope and loss, as those first ancient explorers, I felt small fingers slide into my right hand, seeking comfort from the void, and for a moment, just a moment, I thought it was my stillborn son.

My life to live.

The lights came on, my hand tightened on his, and he smiled up at me, eyes dancing with wonder.

Through new tunnels of dark beauty, the light filtering through prisms of mist, wary of precipices and footing, we began the ascent up out of the earth and rock, to new places that we could only know by arriving in them, feeling the warm wind trickling down from the surface ahead of us, just ahead of us.